ALL THE RIGHT PIECES

"*Following after the events of The Heron Stayed, Chap Smith's life continues in urban Virginia. . . . With a support group of old and new friends, teachers, and an opportunity to meet his sisters separated by distance, Chap matures and approaches adulthood after each new trial.*"
- *The US Review of Books*

ALSO BY JANE S. CREASON

Fiction

When the War Came to Hannah
The Heron Stayed
Conspiracy (with Dr. Edwin M. Swengel)

ALL THE RIGHT PIECES

A Sequel to
The Heron Stayed

Jane Creason

Order this book online at www.trafford.com
or email orders@trafford.com

Most Trafford titles are also available at major online book retailers.

Print information available on the last page.

ISBN: 978-1-4907-7920-1 (sc)
ISBN: 978-1-4907-7919-5 (hc)
ISBN: 978-1-4907-7921-8 (e)

Library of Congress Control Number: 2016920032

Trafford rev. 03/10/2017

 www.trafford.com

North America & international
toll-free: 1 888 232 4444 (USA & Canada)
fax: 812 355 4082

Dedicated to all the wonderful teachers I have known
during my many years in the classroom—
at Danville High School
at Fithian Grade School
at Newtown Middle School
at Danville Area Community College

Chapter 1

Chap's eyes flew open. He lay still, listening—his body tense and sweaty, his eyes blinking as they adjusted to the dark, which was lessened only by the narrow slits of harsh street lighting that peeked through the slated blinds. Something had awakened him.

Moments passed. All was quiet. As his body started to relax and his eyelids droop, he heard a man shout, loud and angry. Then Lou Ella screamed "Don't!" as an object crashed against the thin wall that separated the apartments.

Instantly wide awake, Chap threw back the sheet. Heart pounding, he left his small room, crossed the end of the narrow living room, and moved around the bar that separated it from the kitchen. With his left hand, he felt his way past the pantry door, the stove, the sink, and the refrigerator until he reached the wall behind the dining table.

Several nights before, he'd stood in that same spot, leaning against the wall then as he did now, trying to make out the words as the voice in the apartment next door modulated from a deep growl to an angry yell, but the words were unintelligible.

"Chap?"

He whirled around. His petite, dark-haired, older sister was moving toward him, barely discernible in the faint light from the semicircular glass above the curtained patio door.

"Is he yelling again?" Lori whispered.

"Yes."

Lori moved around the table to join Chap. They huddled together, ears against the wall, as the voice beyond raged. Then the voice became even less distinct as the man moved from the dining area toward the kitchen of the apartment, which was a mirror image of theirs.

"I heard Lou Ella," Lori whispered, "but I haven't heard Owen. He's got to be awake."

When the front door in the other apartment slammed shut, both Lori and Chap started. Then breathing quietly, they listened to the murmur of Lou Ella and Owen's voices for another minute or two. Finally, all was quiet.

"I think they've gone to bed," Lori said softly. "Will you see Owen tomorrow?"

"I plan to."

"Make sure he's okay. Lou Ella, too."

"I will."

After whispering good night, they headed toward their bedrooms. Moving carefully around the sofa and the two stuffed chairs crammed into the living room, Chap reached his bed and crawled beneath the sheet. Unable to relax, he stared at the ceiling and listened to the night sounds, still so unfamiliar to him—the hum of traffic that never seemed to stop on busy Washington Avenue just beyond the apartment complex and the occasional wail of a siren that made the hair stand up on his arms and the back of his neck as he pictured someone hurt or dying or in trouble somewhere. Above him, a baby was crying. Car doors slammed, less often during the night than during the day, but, nonetheless, the noise indicated that at no time was everyone at home and everyone asleep.

During the first week they'd lived in the city, Chap had awakened often during the night, so strange were the sounds. Before that, night had most often been a peaceful time, full of comforting sounds like the occasional creak of a board in the big old house in the Indiana woods, the gentle rustle of leaves when the summer breeze blew, the hoot of an owl, the occasional high yip-yip of a coyote, the patter of rain on the roof, the faint sound of a jet overhead flying toward Indianapolis International, the honking of skeins of migrating Canadian geese, or the mournful cry of a locomotive carried from far away when the wind blew just right. It was late at night when Chap most missed the sounds and the places and the people he'd known all his life with a pain that made his eyes tear.

It was a long time before he slept again.

* * *

The early morning sky was pearly gray. From above came the sounds of scurrying feet and a child's toy playing "Twinkle Twinkle Little Star" over and over again, or maybe it was the alphabet song. Chap couldn't hear the words, only the tinny- sounding notes. Outside, doors slammed in rapid succession, and cars started as people headed for work.

Chap pushed back his empty cereal bowl and reached for the blank paper and pen he'd carried out from his room.

June 19

Dear Erica,

When we decided that we'd handwrite our letters the old-fashioned way, you said that you wanted to picture me writing in all my favorite places—my upstairs bedroom, the clearing in the woods where we spent our last afternoon together, the Church Rock, and the wooden bridge that crosses Wandering River. Who could've imagined when you had to leave First Woods Road that in just six months, so would I? You can't know how I miss all those places and you.

There sure isn't any beauty or romance in the places where I write now. There are exactly eight scrawny trees planted in the complex, all in the median that separates the one-way street which passes our building first and then the other three on our side before looping around at the end and passing the four buildings on the other side.

I can write from the front stoop and stare at the "lovely, tree-lined" street—quotes from the brochure Lori got from the realtor before we moved here. Or I can go to the back "patio," which is in reality a teeny concrete slab with a fake wrought iron rail around it and two hard plastic chairs. Or I can stay in our "clean, cozy" apartment—think of synonyms like sterile *and* claustrophobic. *Or I can go to a bench along the "walking trail in the lovely wooded commons area," which is actually a narrow blacktopped footpath that borders a "woods" about two trees deep. It edges a little creek which is mostly dry already, and it's only mid-June! Are you getting the picture?*

You can't believe the chaos here in the mornings when everyone is trying to leave for work. Eight buildings times three floors in each times four apartments on each floor—even with my shaky math skills, I'd say that adds up to ninety-six apartments. Owen says I should call them "units"—he thinks I'm such a hick. Anyway, each building has a parking lot. That's eight parking lots with two spaces for each apartment. Got the idea of how many cars are coming and going out of the complex? First Woods Road didn't have that many cars travel its four-mile length in six months, maybe even a year! Everyone has to back out of the spaces and pull onto the single lane which circles one-way around the whole complex. Then, at the end, there is no traffic light onto Washington, so people turning left have to wait and wait for traffic to clear and the cars behind stack up. Great planning, wouldn't you say? Lori is now leaving a little after six to avoid the biggest crush that starts about six-thirty. It's easy for her to get out of our lot since we are in the first building, but then she gets stuck as others pour out of the other seven lots and get jammed up at Washington. Makes me glad I don't have my Virginia license yet!

I told you in my last letter that school isn't out yet around here. I see groups of kids of all ages walking out to Washington where I suppose buses pick them up. So far, I haven't met any kids except Owen, who doesn't even go to school.

About ten days ago, when Lori didn't have to go to work until after lunch, we went to the high school to get me registered for fall. Not a good experience. The high school is awful, a huge brick building sitting right on the street with nothing growing in front at all. We had to go through metal detectors to get in, and then we were escorted directly to the administration offices by an armed police officer—no kidding! On the walls and some lockers are gray paint smears which attempt, rather unsuccessfully, to cover graffiti. Kids yell and push in the hallways. I know Riverwoods High wasn't perfect, but it was never like that.

The good news is we left, and I'm NOT registered there—which leads to my next bit of news.

Last weekend, I finally met Douglas's family for the first time—his step-mother and father, one set of grandparents, and his two pesky little sisters who make me glad all my sisters are older. Douglas's step-mother home schooled the girls for several years before she found this private school, which she says is based on a "truly unique educational concept"—her words, not mine. She talked to Lori about me starting school there since I'll likely have to transfer from the high school anyway once Lori and Douglas find a house. I think I wrote you before that the wedding date has been changed from September to November.

Lori and Douglas went to check out the school without even telling me, and they liked it. Tomorrow I'll take the bus there myself like I'll have to do if I decide to go there. I know it's summer, but the school is one of those year-round places. Now here's the really weird part. I get to go free for two weeks so I can decide if I like the school. Have you ever heard of anything so crazy? Would there be any kids at Riverwoods if they got to decide if they liked the school? More about this later!

I'm worried about Owen. Lori and I heard a man yelling from over there again. I mean yelling, really angry and loud. That's twice now. Last time Owen said it was the television I'd heard, but he wouldn't look at me when he said it. I'm going to ask him again today.

Please write me soon. I miss you. I miss you.

Love, Chap

Chap folded the letter and slipped it into the envelope he'd addressed to Erica Anderson in Chicago, Illinois. Opening the front door, he walked through the entry way with the four doors numbered 101 to 104 and the stairway that went to the second and third floors. Tall, multi-paned windows with smudged glass were evenly spaced across the front of the entry way. Outside, Chap walked the short distance to the rows of mailboxes tucked under a roof propped up with four rough-hewn corner posts. He dropped the letter into the outgoing box. It would be hours before the mail—and maybe a letter from Erica—would arrive.

Walking back, he looked at the "unique architecture" featured on the front of the complex brochure. The eight buildings were identical, each a large rectangle made of red brick. Four white, two-story-tall, Southern-plantation-style columns supported a narrow overhang at the top and rested on a narrow concrete porch at the bottom, "gracing" the front of each building. Though Chap was hardly an expert on Southern mansions, such columns, in his opinion, on buildings crammed together along a narrow street with yellow-striped asphalt parking lots separating them looked ridiculous.

The "elegant landscaping" was an aesthetic failure as well. Large barrels of recently planted flowers, which wouldn't likely survive the summer heat since they were drooping already, sat on the ends of each porch. Scraggly shrubs, mulched with shredded bark, were spaced along the front. Maybe, at one point, the effect had been attractive, but now weeds peeked through the mulch, and no one had trimmed the shrubs or removed the dead twigs covered with rusty brown needles. The overall effect was sad, not elegant.

* * *

Back in the apartment, Chap gathered his dirty clothes and stripped the sheets from his bed. Laundry was Chap's preferred chore. For years, they'd had a clear division of labor. He did laundry; Lori did most of the cleaning; they did the cooking and the dishes together. Now, with Lori gone from six a.m. to six p.m., due to the long commute in heavy traffic, Chap was also doing the cleaning, which hardly caused him to break a sweat since the apartment was so tiny. His culinary skills, however, had never progressed much beyond cheese sandwiches, sloppy joes, soup, meatloaf, and tuna casserole. Even so, Lori never complained when there was a meal on the table when she walked in after work. But that morning there was the note he liked to see beneath the lighthouse magnet on the refrigerator: *"Little Brother, I'll cook tonight. Love, Lori."*

Chap routinely complained about the "Little Brother" label, pointing out that at six-feet, the moniker hardly fit anymore. Lori would laugh, her dark eyes sparkling. She'd promise to do better about breaking old habits, but then she'd call him "Little Brother" again in a few days.

Chap stacked the laundry baskets, some hangers, the detergent, a bottle of fabric softener, and the laptop computer into a small cart and headed for the laundry building down by the commons.

The day after they'd arrived, Lori was unpacking the boxes they'd moved in from the rental truck. Most of their furniture had gone to a storage unit since the apartment was furnished. Chap had volunteered to go down to the "spotless, convenient" laundry as soon as he realized the alternative, which was staying there and washing all the dishes before Lori put them into the freshly scrubbed cupboards. Doing the laundry meant having time to read or write while the machines did their jobs. Doing dishes didn't.

That first morning, however, he'd made the mistake of arriving at the laundry building around eleven. The place was filled with cranky little kids and equally cranky mothers who were trying to sort and fold and hang things while their kids ran wild and left sticky, gooey hand prints everywhere as they ate all manner of snacks their mothers had brought to pacify them.

Now Chap arrived early and left before the younger set began to trickle in. Once the front-loading washers were humming and the clothes were tumbling in the suds, Chap got out the laptop. He typed a bit and then stopped to stare at the words on the screen—*Dear Mrs. Hunt.* His hands lay limp in his lap. The words looked strange. He raised his right hand to Delete and watched them disappear. Then he typed a new heading, and within seconds, his fingers were flying around the keyboard.

Journal Entry #1- June 19

Thirteen days in Virginia. Thirteen days of strange noises, too many people, and hot, sticky weather. The shadows on my bedroom ceiling aren't the graceful trees I watched for much of my life when sleep eluded me but harsh lines from the slats that cover my bedroom window.

We have one of the two back apartments on the ground floor of the first building of eight in the complex. The apartment is tiny. Picture a square—half bedrooms and baths and half living room, kitchen, and dining area. The two bedrooms, each with a bathroom and a small closet, open right off the long, narrow living room—no hallway, just a living room wall with two bedroom doors. The front half of the living room is separated from the kitchen by a skinny island counter top with cabinets beneath it. The kitchen consists of a small pantry, a stove, a sink, and a refrigerator all in a row. It's such a tight squeeze between the appliances and the island that Lori and I bump into each other all the time when we are both in the kitchen. The dining area has a small table with a bench and two chairs.

The apartment next door is a mirror image of ours. It's the only other one I've seen inside, but based on the lack of variation on the outside of the eight big buildings in the complex, I'm guessing that all ninety-six apartments are laid out the same way. The furnishings next door are even the same, right down to the fake tree by the front door.

A kid named Owen Barsky lives there—he and his grandma, Lou Ella. He's a strange little character with some sort of disability that makes him hunch to the left and shuffle when he tries to walk short distances. Most of the time, he sits all crooked in a small wheelchair. He talks like he's forty, but his body looks like he's about seven. I think he's probably older than that. It's his teeth. They aren't his baby ones.

His long, narrow face is quite charming with large, dark-gray eyes and a straight nose. His thick straight dark hair hangs onto his forehead with a rakish cowlick that causes one strand to poke up above his right eyebrow. He's serious and intense most of the time.

His grandma is supposed to be home schooling him, but she seems to mostly smoke and doze in a chaise lounge on the little back patio that abuts ours. She hardly looks like a grandma, not that I have any personal experience with grandmothers having never met either of my own. Maybe Owen thinks so too since he calls her Lou Ella instead of Grandma or Nana. Most days she wears tight jean shorts, skimpy tops with skinny straps, and bright-yellow flip-flops.

Not to be mean, but Lou Ella doesn't have the body to wear outfits like that. Her out-of-the-bottle flaming red hair hangs down straight with bangs across her forehead. The hair doesn't match her darkly tanned, wrinkled skin and her dark eyes.

Owen amuses himself by reading an old set of World Book encyclopedias Lou Ella found at a yard sale. Yesterday I got a lecture about Japan—like it's about the size of California but with five times the population. If the Japanese were spread out evenly all across the four main islands, there would be 829 people per square mile. Compare that to First Woods Road where about a dozen people live along its four-mile length! But in Japan, most people can't live anywhere except along the coasts because of all the beautiful mountains and hills, so the population density is really much greater—like 36,000 people per square mile in Tokyo! That would be more people than everybody in Riverwoods crammed into an area that is one mile on each side. Imagine that! It kind of makes our apartment seem spacious. Anyway, since I'm hearing about Japan, I'm guessing Owen's knowledge of the world hasn't progressed beyond J.

I have a job of sorts. Two days after we moved in, Lou Ella hired me to spend a couple of hours a day with Owen to give her "a break," not that she seems to be working all that hard. She says "hired," but I haven't seen any money yet. I go over to his apartment, or he comes over to ours, or we totally escape outside when it's not too miserably hot. He talks a lot, and I mostly listen. He seems starved for someone to pay any attention to him. We also play chess, which he's wicked at. Some days I push his wheelchair to a small park several blocks away. Even with busy Washington Avenue on one side, the park has a peaceful feeling that the housing complex never has.

I also took Owen on the city bus to the public library day before yesterday—a real treat for him since he's never had books of his own choosing before.

Lori got me a bus route schedule and a city map. For a country boy, I've become quite brave in exploring. As I said, I found the library right away along with a used book store, a strip mall with a grocery store, a movie theater, and, most important, a little Mom-and-Pop-type place within walking distance which specializes in homemade ice cream and cookies.

A final thought: When I wrote that autobiographical paper for you last year, I called it "Loss" because I told about losing my mother and three older sisters when I was little. Since then, I've lost the only home I ever knew, the high school and all my friends there, and my father, in a way. It's like I'm losing pieces of my life, one by one, and I don't think I'll find any to replace them in this city.

Since the dryers just stopped, I'll close for now. I really appreciate you letting me write like this.

Chap typed in the email address and hit send.

* * *

Returning to the apartment, Chap put Lori's clothes on hangers into her closet and set the basket on the floor. He'd make her bed later. Then he carried the other basket to his room. In order to put his clothes away, he had to pull the dresser drawers open and then stand at the ends since there was no extra space between the open drawers and the end of his bed. His "nicely furnished" room contained the motel-type basics of a bed, a dresser, a chair, an end table, and a lamp, which, when crammed into the tiny room, were supposed to make it feel "cozy." Moving in the old maple desk that had been in his upstairs room since he was five years old and the big softly-padded leather desk chair from his father's den had caused the squeeze between his bed and the dresser, but he couldn't face even months of living there without something of his own in the apartment. Lori had agreed. She'd added an antique, hand-carved rocker they'd saved from the attic in the old house to her room, causing the same kind of squeeze there. The rest of their possessions, including most of his clothes, were in a storage unit because this minuscule room had a minuscule closet to match.

Chap closed his eyes and tried to imagine the big rooms with high ceilings and lots of windows in the spacious, two-story house in Indiana—the red-flowered wallpaper in the kitchen, the round oak table in the corner, the stone fireplace in the living room with the colorful braided rug in front, the bay window where Lori's pots of violets had bloomed, the wide front stairway in the foyer that led to his sisters' bedrooms and to his which had a view of an open grassy area and a woods beyond.

A series of sharp raps, matching "Shave and a haircut, six bits," ended Chap's reminiscence. Owen's high-pitched voice carried through the thin wall near the dining room table.

"Hey, Chap, you comin' over?"

"In a few minutes," he yelled back.

In the kitchen, Chap grabbed two bananas and some of his favorite snickerdoodles which Lori had baked after work. He liked to think she'd made the treat for him, but reality reared its ugly head. Snickerdoodles were Douglas's favorite cookies as well.

Sometimes Chap tried to make Douglas the villain—the cause of this new life he'd been dragged into—but he couldn't seem to make the black hat fit the tall, good-looking man who made his sister so happy.

Chapter 2

"What do you want to do today?" Chap said, walking into the Barskys' living room.

The two apartments were identical except reversed so that the kitchens were back to back. But if theirs seemed crowded, the Barskys' seemed claustrophobic since two people, Owen and his grandmother, had lived there and accumulated stuff for years, and a third person, Owen's mother, Mollie, appeared and disappeared intermittently as jobs, boyfriends, and finances came and went.

That day Mollie was there, sleeping on a pull-out in the living room with only her straw-colored hair visible beneath a tangle of sheets.

When Chap saw her, he immediately whispered, "I didn't know she was home."

"It's okay," Owen said in a normal tone. "She showed up about 2 a.m., so she won't wake up for a couple of hours yet. How about we take the chess set down to the park since it's not so hot yet?"

"Works for me."

Rolling over pieces of a tabloid scattered on the floor, Owen maneuvered his small wheelchair expertly around the foot of the tan sofa bed and between two stuffed tan chairs. The apartments were all furnished and decorated in a generic tan-beige-ecru-eggshell-white color scheme—a lack-of-color scheme, actually. The walls, the furniture, the countertops, the appliances, the bathroom tile, and the carpet—everything was as drab as a sandy beach minus the sky and the water, everything except for the ceiling-tall, fake, green tree featured in several interior shots in the brochure.

While Owen searched for the chess set inside a tall cabinet, Chap stealthily moved closer to the dining room, feeling like a detective searching for evidence. And there it was. The life-sized, wildly-colored purple and blue ceramic cat, which usually sat on the coffee table, was lying in pieces on the floor. Quickly stepping back to his original spot, Chap watched Owen swivel his chair around and inch back around the furniture.

"We're off," he said, beaming.

Mollie hadn't stirred, and neither had Lou Ella. Only her heavy tanned legs and a haze of exhaled cigarette smoke were visible through the patio screen door.

* * *

At the park, they set up the board and began to play. Owen won the first game handily.

"How'd you learn to play?"

"Mr. Dean—we called him Roger. He was the special needs teacher." Owen paused to stare at the board. "Since when does 'special' mean can't see, can't walk, can't hear, can't read, can't behave," he said, more to himself than to Chap.

Owen moved a man, and Chap could see that he was in trouble again.

"Roger taught me during lunch break. I didn't eat in the cafeteria since I didn't exactly fit in."

"How come you aren't going to school now?"

"Long story short—that's what Lou Ella always says, but the stories are long anyway." A brief grin flashed across his face. Then he frowned. "It was the bullying. They called it 'fun.' It was fun for them but not for me. Roger and the principal tried to help, but duh"—Owen hit himself on the forehead—"like kids are going to bully in front of adults? I don't think so! So when I came home one day with some scratches, Lou Ella said, 'You aren't going back there.' And I didn't."

"What grade were you in?"

"Second. I learned to read in kindergarten, so I sat in a corner with a stack of books and read."

"Reading was all you did?"

Owen shrugged. "Mostly and playing chess."

Then grinning broadly, he declared "Checkmate" again and began to set up the board for another game.

"How come we never talk about you?" he said.

"I don't know. I don't talk a whole lot, I guess. What do you want to know?"

"Your name, for one thing. What kind of name is Chap?"

"An acronym."

Owen frowned.

"Ah, ha. I know something you don't. Chap stands for Charles Henry Anthony Peter. Get it. C for Charles, H for Henry—"

"I got it. Like NASA."

"And scuba."

Owen frowned again.

"Self-contained underwater breathing apparatus," Chap said.

"Neat. It's stuff like that I figure I miss learning at school."

They were silent for a while, concentrating on the game.

"You miss school?"

Owen shrugged. Then he said, "You know, the animals are getting out today."

This time Chap looked puzzled.

"School kids—the animals. Today's the last day."

"Is that so bad? To have other kids around?"

"Gee, Chap, what makes you think they're nicer in the neighborhood than they are at school?"

Chap made a move that was immediately greeted with, "I won again!"

* * *

Later, as they headed back to the complex, Owen said, "Do you live with just your mom? And is that her boyfriend who shows up every few days?"

Chap laughed. "That's my older sister, Lori, and her fiancé, Douglas. Actually, I have four older sisters, but Lori is the only one I know well since the other three left home when I was little."

"And your parents?"

"My mom died when I was a toddler, and my dad . . . ." Chap paused to swallow the lump that threatened to climb into his throat whenever he thought of his father. Then he said, his voice tight and husky, "My dad is in a VA hospital in Illinois. He's very sick."

"Sorry."

They stopped so that Chap could maneuver the chair around a place where tree roots had lifted up one whole section of the sidewalk. They continued, moving slowly since Chap was trying to figure out how to bring up the voice he'd heard during the night.

"What about your dad?"

"I don't know him, not even his name. The story is he came to the hospital, took one look at my twisted body, and split. They weren't married or anything. The court said he had to support me even if he didn't want me, but he doesn't. Lou Ella gripes about having to feed me on the disability check she gets 'cause her back hurts a lot."

Chap stopped at a busy corner to wait for the light to change. Once, on the other side, Owen turned in his chair to look back at Chap. "I think my family is what you call dysfunctional," he said.

Chap tightened his mouth to suppress a grin. What kind of seven or eight or nine or whatever age this kid is knows a word like that? he thought.

"I guess mine is too since I live with a sister, or maybe we're just unusual."

"I think unusual would be better," Owen said softly.

Neither spoke the rest of the way back to the complex. Chap stopped by their mailbox, hoping for a letter from Erica, but the box was empty. Then, taking a deep breath to give himself courage, he moved to the front of the chair and knelt down to face Owen.

"I heard that man again last night."

Owen started to speak, but Chap held up his hand.

"It wasn't the television. I heard his loud voice and a crash. I saw the pieces of the cat when I came to get you."

Owen dropped his eyes. His small body seemed to shrink even smaller.

"Who is he, Owen?"

Owen lowered his head but not before Chap saw the tears well up in his large gray eyes.

"Did he hurt you?"

Owen didn't move.

"Look at me. Did he hurt you?"

"No, he just grabbed my shirt and yelled at me," Owen said without looking up. "That's all."

"But why?" Chap said, fighting to keep his voice normal.

"He drinks," Owen said as he wiped his eyes with his shirt tail.

"That's not a reason."

"For him, it is."

"Owen, who is he?"

Owen sat still, staring down as his hands clasped tightly in his lap.

Finally, Chap rose and moved behind the wheelchair.

"How about some lunch? I have macaroni and cheese," he said.

Owen's head snapped up and around. "I may be younger than you and smaller than you, but I can't be bribed," he said, his eyes flashing angrily.

"Whoa, no need to yell at me. I'm not bribing you. I'm just offering lunch. I'll choose the food. You choose the conversation. Deal?"

Chap stood behind the chair, waiting for Owen to decide. His little dark head was bent down. Suddenly, a small hand darted up over his shoulder.

"Deal," Owen said as Chap shook his hand.

Chap pushed the wheelchair inside. It was pleasantly cool in the kitchen. Owen got out of the wheelchair near the front door and shuffled into the kitchen, holding onto the counter top for support. After they washed their hands, Owen sat down at the dining table.

"How old are you anyway?" Chap asked.

"And you care why?" Owen replied, all bristly again.

"Mouthy little guy, aren't you?" Chap said with a grin.

"Sorry," Owen said, his eyes down, "but I don't like what people say."

"Which is?"

"'You can't be that old!'—as if I don't know how old I am."

"Okay, I need to know if you're old enough to help me cut up some fruit for lunch without chopping off a finger, and I won't say 'You can't be that old.'"

Owen thought a moment and then said, "I was ten on January fifth."

"I thought you were at least fifteen," Chap said, handing him a dish of whole washed strawberries and a paring knife.

"You're a smart you-know-what, but I'm not allowed to say it!" Owen said with a frown.

While stirring the macaroni, Chap could see Owen smiling as he carefully cut the green tops off the strawberries. In short order, Chap ladled the macaroni into one set of bowls, and Owen put halved grapes, banana slices, and strawberries into another set.

After Owen finished a second helping of macaroni, he said quietly, without looking up from his bowl, "His name is Nelson Nelson."

There was a long silence while Chap waited for more information, but Owen said only, "Have you ever heard of a name that ridiculous?"

Chap laughed. "Actually, I have. My friend Tom, the one I told you I punched in the nose the first day we met in sixth grade—his name is Thomas Tom Thompson."

Owen grinned as he pushed back his empty bowl. Then, reaching for a kiwi in the basket of fruit in the center of the table, he asked, "What's this?"

"A kiwi."

"Like the bird?"

"Does it look like a bird?"

"You're being that thing I can't say again!" Owen said, rolling the fuzzy fruit around in his hand. "Seriously, what is it?"

"It's a fruit called a kiwi—same word as the bird, also from New Zealand. Here. I'll cut it in half."

After slicing it in two, Chap showed Owen how to scoop out the soft green fruit as if he were scooping a soft-boiled egg out of a shell. Owen was delighted.

A bit later, Chap asked, "Do you want to tell me any more about Nelson Nelson?"

Owen shrugged and sighed. "I don't know a lot. He's married to Lou Ella, or at least he was before he went to prison. He's on parole now, but he's not allowed to be around kids. Since he can't live with Lou Ella because of me, he sneaks around to see her. He's mad at me because I'm there and mad at Lou Ella for not making me live with Mollie."

"Why was he in prison?"

"I don't know for sure, but I heard Lou Ella tell her friend Sadie he'd hurt somebody real bad."

"Are you afraid?"

Owen stared at his hands again. Chap wasn't sure he'd answer.

Then Owen said in a tiny voice, "He's like two men, a fun grandpa and a scary drunk. There's a knock on the door, and we don't know which one is coming to visit us. The scary one has come only twice, so Lou Ella wants him to come back—the nice one, that is. I think she loves him, and she's waited for him for a long time. She doesn't want this messed up for her, Chap."

"I know, but you can't risk being hurt, Owen. You just can't."

Chapter 3

As Chap waited for the bus the next morning, he thought about what he'd so often thought about the past couple of weeks—his new life and all the missing pieces. Everything had changed. He was starting school only weeks after finishing tenth grade in Indiana. He was waiting for a bus, but there were no trees surrounding the bus stop like those at the end of First Woods Road. Instead, there was a concrete bench with several people sitting on it, and they weren't school kids. The bus approaching from the next block was not yellow but white with a large sign on the side advertising a local news station crew. The passengers were people of all ages and every color. The driver didn't say, "Mornin', Chap," as Tony always had, but she did smile at him.

The vista outside the windows was not a two-lane road with mostly trees on both sides but block after block of shops, apartment complexes, office buildings, and gas stations along with trucks and cars and more cars in the streets, along the curbs, and in the parking lots. The few trees and flowers that flashed by had been planted not by nature but by landscapers.

Chap still felt the need to pinch himself from time to time. He really was living in a city, and he was going to school in late June.

Twenty-five minutes later, he stepped off the bus a block from the school. As he approached the one-story, red-brick building, his heart thudded in his chest. He was tempted to walk back to the bus stop, but after he envisioned telling Lori what he'd done, he kept on walking forward. When he read the sign, The Academy for Mutual Instruction, he wondered what an "experimental" school was anyway. Then he took a deep breath and opened one of the wide front doors.

Nothing about the place looked anything like any school he'd ever seen—not that he'd seen all that many, just Riverwoods Westside Grade School and Riverwoods High School. He'd come to register, yet he was asked to wait for his "guide," who'd been delayed.

So there he was, sitting in a plush blue-green plaid armchair in a cozy-looking corner near the entry doors. He surveyed his surroundings—the drawings on the walls and the lighted glass cabinets full of clay sculptures, all labeled with names and ages; the rug on the floor covered with roads and trees and houses with a tub of small cars nearby; the magazine rack holding copies of *Ranger Rick, Parents, Seventeen, Sports Illustrated, Mother Goose,* and *National Geographic*; coloring books scattered on two small tables; and two brown and white hamsters nibbling breakfast pellets in a big cage nearby.

Beyond the entrance doors was a circular counter with four computer keyboards around it. In the center of that area were several people manning phones and computers and greeting those entering. It had been one of those— "Call me Miss Celia," she'd said—who'd apologized to Chap for the wait.

Settled in the chair, Chap watched the procession of people entering. A tiny dark-haired girl pulled a box from the waiting area over to one of the computers. Then she clambered up on it, leaned over to study the keyboard, and with one chubby finger punched in four letters.

"I type it my ownself, Miss Celia," she said.

Miss Celia walked over to the screen. "You sure did, Angel," she said as the little girl climbed off the box.

Chap counted five letters in Angel. Miss Celia winked at him and mouthed, "She left out the *e.*"

Following Angel to the keyboard were two boys about eight, twins maybe, who also typed and then headed for separate doors visible on the back side of the center. Then an elderly couple entered, typed in their names, and disappeared behind the first door on the right. Next came a young woman carrying a sleeping toddler.

"I'll check Mikey in," said Miss Celia. "You go on down to the nursery."

The nursery? Chap thought, even more convinced it was a mistake for him to be there. As he rose to leave, a voice called from beyond the center area.

"Hey, I think you're waiting for me. Sorry that I'm a bit late, but I couldn't quit what I was doing in the middle of things, you know. I'm Branson. What's your name?"

All of that poured out of a small boy with a round freckled face capped with rust-colored straight hair that hung down to the top of his round glasses. He pushed his glasses up farther onto his nose and added, "Let's get this show on the road."

He turned on his heel and started off around the central area. He'd moved several yards away before he turned and said, "Are you with me or not? I'm guide this week. You need to be guided. It's that simple. And you still haven't told me your name."

"It's Chap."

"All right, Chap. Let's get this tour thing done."

With that, he strode off again, Chap following closely behind. For a little guy, he sure could cover a lot of ground in a hurry. In a rapid-fire manner, Branson began his tour spiel. As they passed doorways, starting on the left and moving around the circular area, he described the school's layout.

There were four very large rooms opening off the circular hallway which was bright with art work on all the walls and sky lights every few feet. Each one was a specialty room, called a center, for language arts, math, science, and social studies. Each was arranged to allow lots of activities to be going on at the same time with individual study areas, books shelves of all kinds, computers, chairs and tables of all sizes, and lab equipment—all the stuff one expects to see in any school but not in the usual rooms with twenty or thirty student desks and a teacher's desk up front. Each center had glassed-off office space.

People were moving around everywhere—little kids, big kids, and adults of all ages. Once again, Chap considered interrupting Branson and heading back to the bus stop.

"Here's the cafeteria area. You hungry?"

"At ten o'clock?"

"Yeah, are you hungry at ten o'clock? If you are, you can follow me to the fruit and snack area. Milk and juice are over here, too. If you aren't, you can watch me eat," Branson said, reaching for a cranapple juice and a granola bar.

After Chap chose the same, they sat down at a nearby table with six chairs. Other people were scattered around the room which had colorful murals of mountain scenes and seascapes painted on the walls. Two girls, clad in bright blue aprons, walked from table to table as people left, spraying and wiping each one clean. The smell of vegetable soup came from the kitchen area behind the hot bar.

"The way this works," Branson said between bites of granola, "is that you get to come here for two weeks to see if you like it. It's best that the older students make the choice themselves. The ones under eight—well, their parents generally decide. Your family has paid a little bit for you to eat here and start work, but you won't really register until you decide if you want to stay. Clear?"

Branson stood up and gathered up his trash. Chap followed.

Assuming that Chap's silence meant he understood, Branson continued, "Let's peek into the gym area and the Art and Music Centers. Then I'll take you to your homeroom teacher. I'm a bit pushed for time since I'm due to help Emily soon, but I'm in your homeroom, so I'll see you everyday.

"How'd you get a name like Chap, anyway?" he said over his shoulder as he hustled toward the music room.

Chap explained the acronym thing as he had done so many times in his life. Then he asked, "How'd you get a name like Branson?"

"That story is a bit more unusual than an acronym. My parents are archeologists at the Smithsonian. They hadn't been able to have a kid for years, finally deciding that fate meant for them to be childless. Then, to celebrate both their fortieth birthdays, they decided to take a long trip through the United States, which included a stop in Branson, Missouri." With a self-satisfied smile, he added, "Well, you know what happened there."

After finishing the tour, they headed back toward the central area, which was called the Command Center, and the first room on the left, the Language Arts Center, where Branson handed Chap off to one of the three adults there—a tall, slender, dark-skinned lady with black hair pulled back in a bushy ponytail. Her long loose denim jumper barely cleared her sandals, which were decorated with large colorful rhinestones.

"I'm Miss Sydney," she said, extending her hand. "You'll be in my homeroom if that's all right with you. Your sister said your favorite subject is English, so it made sense to start you here."

Chap nodded as he surveyed the room. There was activity everywhere and a low hum of voices. Pairs of older and younger kids sat around tables or on the floor in beanbag chairs. One larger group of about a dozen small kids surrounded a gray-haired man who sat next to an easel covered with brightly colored cards. Along one wall were carrels filled with older kids—some wearing head sets, some using computers, and some reading.

"Did Branson explain the two-week trial?"

Chap nodded again.

"What we'll do is figure out a general schedule for you today. Then you can start work or come back tomorrow. It's up to you."

They walked into the office space where Miss Sydney sat down at a computer. She had a copy of his Riverwoods transcript lying beside it. She began asking Chap questions about his goals for school, his best and worst subjects, and even his household skills.

"Let's see," she said as she began to type. "You'll be a senior."

"No, I'm only a junior."

She grinned. "Not really. Here you'll be a senior. That means you'll be working to finish high school requirements and to prepare for college. We group kids loosely. We call the tiny ones "babes" for about two years. Once they're mobile, they're "little ones" for the next two or three years. Referring to them as preschoolers doesn't sound right since this is a school, and they're already here. When they begin reading and writing and doing basic math, we call them "beavers," like eager beavers. Once they're independent readers, we call them "sponges" because they soak up lots of content-related material. We have lots of sponges enrolled here. You seniors are capable of independent learning. Your first goal is to meet high school graduation requirements, but you can also take on-line college courses and pursue areas of special interest to you."

Miss Sydney looked at Chap's records from Riverwoods High School again.

"You'll need help, it seems, with math, and you'll likely need to spend extra time on it in order to get in the three required classes for graduation. You've had algebra, but you'll need more than that. Understand?"

Chap only nodded.

"Now, let's get you a schedule."

Activities that required groups or were age-related were scheduled first. He chose basketball for his physical activity. He played no instrument nor sang, so his music would be an on-line class, American Music Appreciation. Since his strong subjects were reading and writing, they decided that he'd take a combination course relating early American history and literature from the colonial period through the Civil War. For biology, he chose a unit in ornithology. He didn't tell Miss Sydney why he chose to study birds. He'd continue studying Spanish. Finally, he was signed up for math, which was not his choice but something he knew he needed.

By the time the schedule was finished, he knew he'd be spending most of each day working on his own in the different centers and an hour playing basketball. He'd have a student tutor in the Math Center.

"It's called Mutual Instruction. We shorten that to the initials, pronounced 'em eye.' It means that kids help kids," Miss Sydney explained.

Part of each day he'd also help with chores at the school, starting with doing the laundry from the kitchen and the nursery. Later, after he'd completed tutor training, he'd help a few younger kids, probably with reading. That's where the mutual part of the instruction came into being.

"Now, I'm sure the most important thing for a growing young man is food. The cafeteria is open all day long. Families pay a food allowance and kids simply eat when they're hungry or need a break. My guess is that Branson has already taken you there since he's a notorious empty pit. In the morning, there are cereals, yogurt, hard-boiled eggs, toast, and fruit—hot oatmeal when it's cold. That's my favorite. Then snacks are available before and after lunch, which is hot food from about eleven to one. If there are groups working or practicing during the evening, there are sub sandwiches available in the refrigerator. Eat when you want to."

Chap just stared at her. This place was so weird.

"I know. Strange school, huh? Why don't you walk around by yourself for a while. Go into the other centers. Introduce yourself to the math instructor. That'll be Miss Erin. She'll get you set up with a tutor there since math isn't your strong area. Then go to science. Mr. Ivan will show you the material for the bird study unit."

When Miss Sydney asked if he had questions, Chap continued to stare.

She grinned. "That's often the reaction I get. Here, let me show you how we keep track of you all."

She walked to the computer near the wide doors that led into the hallway. "I have you listed in my homeroom. When you come into the building each day, you'll type your name into a computer at the Command Center. That registers you for the day—kind of like employees who clock in and out of work. Our students do have to meet minimal attendance requirements set by the state. We just aren't as picky about when they are here.

"After you check in there, you come here. Since not everyone comes to school at the same time, the homeroom meeting lasts for half an hour or so with kids coming and going. We share major news with our homeroom group and then post it on the message board. We check for schedule changes, and then everyone heads off to work. Whenever kids leave homeroom, they indicate where they're going. I can track all of my group."

She pulled up a screen. Nine were in the math room, three in the gym, four in girls' chorus, two at the restroom, two working in the cafeteria, two outside working in the flower gardens . . . . The list went on.

"Here, I'll list you touring. Then when you get to math, you can sign in there."

"If there's a power failure, the kids can all go home, and no one will ever know," Chap said with a grin.

Miss Sydney laughed. "Not quite. See that long bulletin board with all the names on it. It's magnetized. All the kids have tags they take with them and put on the boards where they are and they write in here where they've gone. Some times we have power out drills. The kids think it's a hoot! Even the beavers can print RR for restroom or C for cafeteria or M for math."

Chap was even more certain this was the weirdest place he'd ever seen.

* * *

Chap chose to remain that first day. He met Miss Erin, who looked as Irish as her name with pale skin, green eyes, and black hair parted in the middle and hanging straight to her shoulders. She was inches shorter than Chap. Mr. Ivan, in the Science Center, looked like he'd be more comfortable on a ranch than in a city school. His narrow, deeply lined face was capped with bristly gray hair. He wore a red-and-white-checked, Western-style shirt, tucked into Levis which were held up by a wide leather belt and a huge buckle shaped like a cowboy hat.

Then Chap wandered around to see what else was going on besides what he'd seen in the three centers he'd already visited. He listened to a swing band rehearsal awhile, watched a group play dodge ball in the gym, and helped carry some flats of flowers for a group planting a shade garden outside. He stepped into the huge library that was full of kids at tables and in easy chairs and tiptoed past the nursery door on which hung a huge sign that said, "Quiet—sleeping babes." He ate lunch when he was hungry. Then he checked back into the Language Arts Center. There he found out that it was his choice how much work, if any, he'd take home each day.

"At first, you'll decide how hard you want to work and how fast you want to proceed through the units," Miss Sydney said, "but if it looks like your progress isn't close to what it should be, you'll get some suggestions about what you should be doing both here and at home."

"That actually works?"

She nodded. "Yes, it really does for the most part. Let me tell you more about the Academy. It's only five years old. We started with about fifty kids, mostly twelve and younger. Once the system was set up with the kids helping each other a lot, the atmosphere became learning oriented. There was no war between faculty and kids, no fear of failing, and no severe rules to rebel against. Later that year and during the second year, about a hundred more kids came in, and they got absorbed into that atmosphere. We've got over three hundred here now with room for twice that many."

Chap tried to picture his friend Tom and the lunchroom table gang at RHS at the Academy and couldn't. They basically tolerated school and didn't get into trouble much, but none did more than what was absolutely necessary to pass, and sometimes that was with just a D.

When Chap left around three that afternoon, he chose to take home the first unit in the American literature course, a collection of sermons by Puritan ministers, and a booklet Miss Sydney gave him about the past, present, and future of the Academy. He didn't take home any math.

Chapter 4

The next day, Wednesday, Chap arrived to a welcoming ceremony in homeroom for both himself and a lanky seven-year-old with large blue eyes, pale skin, and short kinky-curly hair so blonde it looked almost white. Both boys walked down a line, getting high-fives from everyone— at least Chap got high-fives. The little kid walked the line with his eyes straight ahead and his hands clenched into fists at his side. At the end of the line was a basket of freshly baked peanut butter cookies. Chap took two. The other kid took none.

When asked to do so, Chap introduced himself by explaining his name, describing the big old house in the woods in Indiana, and identifying his favorite free-time activities as reading, running, and writing letters.

The seven-year-old introduced himself by yelling, "You *can't* call me Donald, you *can't* call me Donnie or Don, you *can't* call me Eugene, and you *can't* call me Gene. And I don't like to do nothin'!"

After the cookies disappeared, the day began. One group of young beavers joined Mr. Bob to work on a program called YAK Phonics. Chap had watched part of that the day before. It was some sort of story that introduced letter-shaped things, such as a curve in the road that looked like a C and started with the "ku" sound. Several groups of two or three small kids sat with bigger kids and read. Miss Sydney was working with some beavers with dictionaries and vocabulary cards. Other kids checked out on the computers by the door and headed for other centers. Most of the older students like Chap went to the carrels to work on their own units. Soon Chap was immersed in the history of the Puritans—their beliefs, their motivations, and their life style.

The new kid refused an offer to join the YAK group or the reading groups. Instead, he sat in an over-sized purple beanbag chair with his arms folded and his face set in stony defiance. Miss Sydney assured him that he was welcome to sit if that was his choice, adding that there was only one rule at the Academy—that no one could do anything to keep others from learning.

That's where he still was when Chap returned later that morning from playing a fast and furious game of basketball in the gym and from taking some diagnostic tests in the Math Center.

About noon, Miss Sydney motioned Chap into the glassed-off area.

"As you might guess," she said, "our new little guy isn't here of his own free will. He recently became a foster child. His foster mom is Miss April, who works with the little ones. She and her husband, Allan, were part of the group of parents who got the school organized. We had their two older sons here first and now their foster children.

"Anyway, I noticed him watching you while you were here reading, and he seemed to brighten up a bit when you returned just now. As I explained yesterday, we don't train anyone to become a tutor for several weeks, but I'm wondering if you'd let him tag along with you to lunch and anywhere else he won't be a bother—assuming he'll even move out of that chair."

"I'll try."

After he left the office, Chap paused by the purple beanbag and said, "Hey, other new kid, want to go eat?"

With that simple inquiry, Chap gained a shadow who followed him to lunch and then to get the instructions about doing the laundry; the kid sat in the bleachers when Chap played basketball the next day; he sat nearby when Chap worked on math; and he sat close enough to Chap to see a video about hummingbirds one day and another one about other birds that act as pollinators the next.

"I'm not going to do nothin'," he'd say each time they went to a new center.

"I know," Chap would answer, "but maybe you'll like doing nothing in a new environment."

* * *

Owen wanted to know everything about the Academy. He knocked on the wall a little before eight on Saturday morning, asking if he could come over.

Lori, her hair all mussed, was sitting at the table in a nightgown and a pale blue robe, reading the *Washington Post* and drinking a cup of coffee, when he wheeled himself into the apartment.

"How goes, Owen?" she said, glancing up from the paper.

"Fine, Miss Lori, but I liked it better when Chap wasn't at school."

Lori laughed. "He's deserted you, huh?"

Owen shrugged and moved toward the front bedroom where Chap was smoothing the quilt on his bed.

"You're up early," Chap said.

"I thought we might go to the park to talk before it gets too hot."

"Sorry, but I don't have time since Douglas is coming around ten to take us to look at some houses nearer where they work."

Looking down at his hands, which were clasped in his lap, Owen said quietly, "I guess you'll be moving some day."

"Yes, but not today. They aren't getting married until November."

Chap paused while Owen seemed to shrink in his chair.

"Hey, cheer up. We've got some time before I have to shower. How about some breakfast? I'm hungry."

In short order, Chap had scrambled eggs, rye toast, and halved kiwis ready for the three of them.

Between bites, Owen fired question after question about that "new-type" school. He wanted to know everything—what the centers looked like, how the kids behaved, what the teachers were like, what they ate for lunch, what it was like to have a snack at any time, and what the little kids did during outside recess. Owen looked puzzled about there being no classrooms for kids of the same age.

"You really are in the same room with six-year-olds?"

"I am. Some even younger than six. Miss Sydney says that when there are more kids in the school, they plan to have a separate center for the kids first learning to read, write, and do math. But at this time, we're all together. Actually, I'm trying to help a new seven-year-old adjust to school right now."

Chap went on to tell about his days with the new no-name kid. Owen had trouble understanding how anyone wouldn't want to learn how to read.

"What's wrong with that kid?" he asked.

"I don't know, but his life can't have been easy if he's a foster kid now."

Owen asked more questions as Lori quietly listened to Chap's description of the Academy. It was good to see his relaxed face as he talked to Owen.

Later, after Owen left, Lori said, rather sadly, "If I ever saw a kid who needed to go to school, that is one."

* * *

On Monday, Chap's shadow sat in the purple beanbag chair, arms crossed and eyes straight ahead, while Chap continued his study of the Puritans. But when Chap checked out to go to the gym, the little guy once again checked out and followed him the rest of the day.

On Tuesday, Chap saw him watching the YAK group. On Wednesday, he vacated the purple beanbag chair and took a yellow one closer to the group. On Friday, Chap discovered him drawing letters *c* like the curve, *s* like a snake, *t* like a tree, *y* like the horns of the yak, and *b* like a bat and ball. The kid was learning the alphabet and the sounds on his own. However, he refused Miss Sydney's suggestion that he join the group.

"Baby stuff," he said loudly, his nose all wrinkled up in distaste.

That was true in a sense since the young beavers did look like "babies" compared to him. He was half again as tall and two or three years older than most in the group.

The next Monday morning, as they folded clean kitchen towels, Chap said bluntly, "I need a name for you besides 'Hey you.'"

"Well, you *can't* call me Donald and you *can't* call me Don—"

"Yeah, yeah, I heard that speech the first day. What's so wrong with those names, anyway?"

"They left me," he said with a deep frown.

"Who left you?"

"My dad and my granddad."

"Left how?"

"Dead and just gone is how."

"Ah, and were their names Donald and Eugene?"

The kid stared at his hands, head down, like Owen had done when Chap asked about Nelson Nelson.

"You don't want to be called by their names," Chap said softly.

The kid sat without moving. Chap rose to get a piece of paper from a scratch pad lying on the kitchen counter. As the kid watched, Chap printed out Charles, then Henry underneath that, then Anthony below Henry, and Peter at the bottom.

"Those are my names," he said. "I have four because my father wanted me to be named after him, Charles Henry, and my mother wanted me to be named after her father, Anthony Peter, since I was born on his birthday."

Chap drew a downward oval, circling CHAP. He took off his name badge and laid it next to the circled letters.

"See how I got the nickname Chap?"

Chap printed Donald with Eugene beneath it, pronouncing each name as he did so. Then he circled DE.

"How would you like to be called De? De Ellison. How does that sound?"

For the first time, the bit of a smile that Chap had seen only a few times turned into a wide beam. By day's end, there was no one at the Academy who didn't know that "No-name" Ellison was now De Ellison.

* * *

July 4ᵗʰ in Virginia

Hey, Tom, how goes? You'll never guess what I've been doing the past couple of weeks. I've been testing out a school called AMI, the Academy for Mutual Instruction. Yes, I really got to try it out to see if I liked it. Now I'm officially registered. I know it's July, but the school runs almost all year round. Kids don't have to go more than the required number of days, but I hear that most do. They can take off whenever they want to. The school is closed only three times a year—two weeks in early August, two weeks for the Christmas-New Year's holidays, and two weeks around Easter.

I'll say "weird" here once. Then you can say it whenever you want to!

There are no classrooms with rows of kids' desks or teachers' desks. No bells, no set times for much of anything. I go to the gym at 9:00 to play basketball with a dozen other senior guys—yes, I'm a senior! The rest of the day I work on my own—literature and history with lots of writing involved, an ornithology unit in biology—look that one up, buddy—music appreciation on-line, Spanish, and math. I'm responsible for doing one or two loads of laundry each day, kitchen towels and blankets from the nursery. Yes, I said nursery. I stick in a load, set a timer, and go back to my studies. When the timer dings, I run back to put the load into the dryer. A good study break!

I'll be a tutor soon since I'm almost done with the training. I'll probably help a little guy in my homeroom who rarely smiles. He's a foster kid. He tags along after me every day, so Miss Sydney, my homeroom teacher, thinks I may be the one to break through his shell.

Now listen to this. I can go to the cafeteria to eat whenever I want to. I can see your mouth open from here!

What I really wanted to tell you about is math. You know me and math. Without your help last year, I probably would've flunked algebra. Here I took a pre-test in fifteen separate areas, working both computation and story-type problems, all the way from basic adding and multiplying to working with fractions and percentages and then on to algebra. What showed up were the holes in my skills. For example, I can add just fine, but I have trouble with long division. We can't use calculators until we prove we can do calculations quickly and accurately. Now I'm not in a particular math class like advanced algebra or geometry. Instead, I'm working on the areas I'm weak in with a student tutor, a math whiz like you. More about her later. When I feel comfortable, I take a test on the computer and either work on that area more or move on to the next hole in my skills. When the holes are filled, I'll pick up algebra again to review and then move on to geometry.

When I think back to one year ago, I can hardly believe that my life has changed so much. A year ago today, I was probably reading a book under the big maple tree near the Church Rock above Wandering River, Lori was working in Riverwoods, and my father was in his den as always, writing his book—or so we thought. One year later, my father is in a VA hospital in Illinois, Lori will marry Douglas soon, and I'm living in a city in Virginia and going to an experimental school in the summer, no less. Life sure is weird sometimes!

I sure wish I was there with you guys to see the fireworks down by the river.

Your buddy, Chap

P.S. I talked to Erica last night. She says to tell you hi.

Chapter 5

Chap sat in the Math Center, nervously bouncing his pencil on the blank math paper in front of him. As his tutor, Jean Marie, approached, his stomach knotted.

Weeks before, when Miss Erin had first told him that he'd be working with a girl named Jean Marie, he'd pictured someone his age, maybe a blonde with blue eyes who liked pastel colors and white sandals. The name suggested femininity. Instead, Jean Marie looked as if she'd slid off the back of a Harley in front of the Academy. She was tall and very slender. Her black hair was spiked in all directions. The black lipstick matched the black fingernails and the dark lines around her brown eyes, all in sharp contrast to her pale skin. Chap was soon to learn that her daily uniform was black jean shorts with a loose black tee and high-top black sneakers with a pair of socks—a different bright color each day—peeking over the shoe tops.

Her manners seemed as bold as her appearance. The first day she'd said abruptly, "I'm Jean Marie. I hear you're Chap."

She paused while she looked him over from head to toe. Then she asked, "How old are you?"

"Sixteen."

"I'm going on sixteen," she said. "Let's get started filling in the holes in your math skills."

With that, she grabbed a little bag from one of the tubs under the big windows and dumped out a lot of colored rods and cubes, identifying them with a word that sounded like "queeze in air." It wasn't long before Chap was totally involved with the concept of place value, understanding for the first time why he added up the first column and then if it was ten or more, put a number over the second column before adding that column. He'd always just done that because he'd been told to do so. The same was true with borrowing when subtracting.

By the end of the first session, he had to admit that it was fun to know the why and not just the how of something as simple as adding and subtracting. Jean Marie really did know how to explain things.

During the next lessons, he learned the whys of the multiplication and division processes.

"This is neat," Chap said as more and more made sense. "You're good!"

Maybe that small compliment was what started the problem.

Several days later, Jean Marie pulled her chair up much closer to Chap's. Two days after that, she let her knee touch his leg and her hand touch his hand. Then the next day, it was her shoulder brushing up against his. Chap kept inching away, but she kept moving closer.

Chap did a double take when Jean Marie walked into the Math Center for their next session. Her hair was brushed down in an uneven bob, actually shiny and clean-looking. The black makeup was gone, replaced with soft coral lipstick and matching fingernail polish. She wore a modest pale-pink sleeveless dress. Only the black high-tops remained of the first Jean Marie, but the socks peeking over the tops were pale pink to match the dress. As soon as she sat down, Chap also knew she'd dumped on the perfume.

"You look different, Jean Marie."

"You like it?"

"I guess I do."

But when she moved close and put her hand on his thigh, he jerked back.

"What's the matter with you?" she hissed, her face all tight and red.

"What do you mean?"

"I mean are you gay or something?"

It was Chap's turn to blush. The silence got long as he stared at her.

Finally, he whispered, pronouncing each word distinctly, "I like girls just fine. As a matter of fact, I have a girlfriend—if that's any of your business."

"Yeah, which one?" she said with a sneer, looking around the center as if one of the girls there might have a sign on her back saying, "Chap's girl."

"Not here. In Chicago."

"You're just telling me that."

Chap reached into his back pocket and pulled out his billfold. Slowly, he took out a picture of Erica.

"What happened to her?" Jean Marie exclaimed as she peered at the scar which ran from Erica's left temple to the bridge of her nose.

"She was run down by a drunk driver."

The silence at the table got long again. Then Jean Marie rose and fled from the room.

With his hand shaking, Chap picked up his pencil and finished the worksheet, but he didn't return to the Math Center for the next three days.

In homeroom the following day, Miss Sydney said, "You need to see Miss Erin before you start your literature work."

Chap didn't protest. He simply rose, signed out, and slowly walked to the Math Center. When he got to the door, he was relieved to see that Jean Marie wasn't there. Miss Erin motioned him to come to her office.

"I'll get right to the point, Chap," she said. "You need math—a lot of math—and for some reason, you've quit working on it. I know the Academy allows you kids a lot of freedom to handle your time and your work, but not working at all is unacceptable."

Chap stared down at his hands.

"We rely on kids' honesty here. Obviously, there's a problem. I can't help if you don't help me understand."

Talking truthfully to teachers was not the usual teen code—at least, it hadn't been at Riverwoods High School, but everything at the Academy was different. Unlike the other guys he knew at RHS, he'd trusted Mrs. Hunt when he was troubled many months ago. He decided to trust Miss Erin now.

"Jean Marie is interested in more than math," he said, trying to be tactful.

Miss Erin said nothing, looking as if she expected him to say more, so he did.

"She sort of came on to me, and I finally had to show her a picture of my girlfriend to get her to think I wasn't—"

Chap stopped short. He knew his face was red. "Well, you know," he added.

"Ah," Miss Erin said with a slow smile. "Our Jean Marie has discovered boys."

"Just now?"

"Well, yes, she's still young."

"She's going on sixteen," Chap said.

Miss Erin's smile turned into a wide grin. "Oh, yes, she's going on sixteen after she gets to fourteen and then fifteen."

"She's only thirteen!" Chap exclaimed.

"That she is."

"But she's so smart."

"That she is, too."

They didn't talk for a bit.

"When there's a problem," Miss Erin said quietly, "we like for you kids to handle it yourselves if you can. Were you doing well with Jean Marie's math help?"

"Yes."

"So it's a matter of getting her to accept you as her tutee without hurting her newly found femininity. Think you can do that?"

Chap hesitated. Then he said, "I'll try."

He figured that he sounded a whole lot more confident than he felt.

* * *

So there he was, nervously bouncing his pencil, as the once-again "black" Jean Marie approached, her hair looking even spikier than before. Even her socks were black.

When she sat down—this time on the opposite side of the table—Chap said, "I didn't mean to hurt your feelings. You're a great tutor. I'm just taken if you're looking for a boyfriend. I really love Erica."

That was a long speech for Chap. He'd practiced it over and over before falling asleep the night before.

Jean Marie looked at him thoughtfully then said, "I lied. I'll be fourteen next month."

"I know."

"Okay. I'll accept your apology. Now it's my turn. I shouldn't have called you gay, and I shouldn't have been so forward about how your girl looks. You really love her?"

"I do, but I wasn't nice to Erica when I first talked to her, and I hurt her feelings. I don't want you to feel the way she did. It was a long time before we became friends. So are you okay, Jean Marie?"

"I am," she said quietly, "but I'd like to know what makes Erica so special. Will you tell me more about her?"

"I will."

And he did after they went to the cafeteria for a snack. Chap told her about the first time Erica had tried to talk to him. He was jogging home on First Woods Road, and she was riding her bike to make her leg stronger. He was upset that she'd caught a mistake in a paper he'd written for English—telling the teacher that the bird he'd written about was a heron and not a crane. Erica tried to talk to him, but he didn't look at her. When she told him about being hit by a drunk driver, he said only, "Too bad," in a distinctly sarcastic tone even though he hadn't intended for it to sound that way. After she angrily asked him what his problem was, he said that he didn't talk much to anyone. She said, "That excuses rudeness perfectly," in a distinctly sarcastic tone, which he was certain was intentional, and pedaled away.

Chap paused then added, "We saw each other every day at school, but we didn't speak to each other for two more months."

"You were a real jerk."

"You don't have to be quite that honest, Jean Marie," Chap replied with a bit of a frown.

"So how'd you get together?"

"She asked if she could help me one day when my dad left our car on the road and I couldn't find him."

"Why did he do that?"

"I didn't know why then, but I do now. He has Alzheimer's disease."

"What did Erica do after that day?"

Chap shrugged. "She was just there—when things were good or things were bad."

Jean Marie rose and picked up their juice bottles. When she returned, she sat a moment before asking, "Why is Erica in Chicago?"

"She had to have more surgery on her leg because it hadn't healed right."

"Do you see her often?"

"No, not since last May, but we write letters every week and talk on the phone some times."

"Why not every day?"

"That was her idea. Since we're so far apart, she thinks we need to meet other people and make new friends. She says that if our love is real, it'll be strong when we can be together again."

"Do you believe that?"

Chap shrugged again. "I hope she's right. We're already talking about college. I'm hoping that if we don't go to the same one, we'll at least be going to ones in the same state."

Jean Marie broke the seriousness of the moment with a laugh. "Well, if you're planning to go to college, we'd better get started on your less than sterling math skills. You know, math skills equal math credits equal earning a high school diploma equals getting accepted into college."

Chap grinned at her as they walked back to the Math Center.

When Jean Marie again sat on the opposite side of the table, Chap laughed. "Do you really want to read everything upside down? You can sit on this side again."

"Okay, Chap," she said as she took the chair beside him. "Now how do you plan to solve the first problem?"

Chap had a math tutor again. When he glanced toward the office, he made a quick okay sign to Miss Erin, who was smiling at him through the glass.

Chapter 6

The washers were all filled and the quarters fed into the slots. No one else was in the laundry room that Saturday morning. Actually, the entire complex was quite peaceful at seven a.m. The early morning sun was not yet beating down. Chap took his laptop outside to a nearby concrete bench and began to type.

Journal Entry #3 - July 15

Last time I wrote about the weird school I'm attending. I'll add only that I'm enjoying my days there. I like working independently on the American literature-American history course; I'm making good progress in math with my strange tutor—I'll save her for entry #4 maybe—and I'm feeling really good about tutoring that angry little kid I wrote you about, the one I nicknamed De. He's finally smiling once in a while and learning the alphabet by eavesdropping on a phonics group in the Language Arts Center, believe it or not!

What I really want to tell you about is my bus ride, actually not the ride so much as the people. I've always believed that people in cities are quite impersonal and rarely as neighborly as they are in Indiana. If I had to pass judgment based on our housing complex, I'd say that opinion is correct. We've lived here about six weeks, and we know nobody's names except for Owen and Lou Ella next door. We say hello to the family upstairs when we run into them, but that's about it. If I speak to people at the mail boxes, they rarely speak back.

On the other hand, there's the bus. Miss Dorothea is the main driver. She's heavy-set, about forty, I'd say, since her oldest kid is in high school. She has shiny dark skin, a short reddish Afro, and laugh lines at the corners of her eyes. I see her the most since drivers have a four-days-on and two-days-off schedule so that no one always has to work weekends.

The fourth day I rode the bus, Miss Dorothea said, "Well, if you're going to be one of my regulars, I'd better get to know you."

From then on, she managed to get my life history in bits and pieces, which she remembers down to each detail—along with the histories of all the other regulars. There's twenty-eight-year-old Julie, who works in the Parks Department and who is separated from her husband; Grandpa Ben, who walks with a cane and takes the bus every day to a little café; Thomas and Michael, freckle-faced ten-year-old twins, who go to a Catholic grade school near the Academy; Andy, who seems to be homeless—he's unshaven and quiet and mostly sleeps. I've seen her give him a dollar or two. She gives advice to Patty, who is expecting her first baby in mid-August. She gets off the bus to help frail Mrs. Johanson up the steps. I don't know all the regulars, but Miss Dorothea sure does. If someone isn't at a stop, she asks if anyone knows if he or she is sick. And we all know about Miss Dorothea's experiences with her husband and four kids!

The point is the bus is a community in a bustling city where most of the time I feel alone. I still miss country living. Even though I was alone a lot there with Lori working and my father isolated in his den, I was not lonely. Here it is easy to feel lonely because I can see and hear people all the time, yet I have a connection with almost no one. Maybe people don't form attachments when they're likely to be leaving soon. There are moving vans around the complex all the time—no small wonder since who'd like to live in those boxy, crowded apartments long-term?

Since I work independently a lot at school, you might think I feel isolated there, but that isn't the case. As I said before, I like the history-literature course; the music appreciation class on-line is great, and I'm now studying with a partner for the bird unit in biology. We're going to walk a neighboring park together next week to do a bird survey. All in all, we're even more connected with each other there since we work together a lot. If you think about it, a group of twenty-five sitting in rows and mostly not talking— or talking one at a time—isn't exactly being together.

Thanks again for letting me write to you. You were the best part of RHS for me.

P.S. I haven't figured out why you're willing to read one more "paper" from a student.

* * *

Owen was sitting in the lobby when Chap returned to the apartment building.

"I heard you leave early," Owen said. "Can I come in with you now?"

"Sure."

It seemed to Chap that Owen was more eager every day to hear about school. He wanted to know all about De, especially if he was beginning to read. He was also following Chap's studies—looking up various birds he was learning about in the ornithology unit and some of the authors he was reading in the literature course. He'd read all the encyclopedia articles about Increase and Cotton Mather, Anne Bradstreet, the Salem witchcraft trials, and Puritanism.

But what Owen most wanted to know about was math. During his brief time in public school, he'd learned to count and to add and subtract single digit numbers—nothing more.

Owen's plaintive statement that morning, "I need to learn math, but how?" stayed with Chap all weekend.

* * *

On Monday morning, Chap checked out to go see Miss Erin as soon as homeroom was over. De tagged along as usual. In a rush, Chap told her all about Owen—his crooked body, his little wheelchair, his ability to read an encyclopedia but his lack of math skills.

"Can I take home some math papers and maybe the Cuisenaire rods to help him a little?" he asked.

"Sure. Just bring the rods back each day since we use them so much."

She paused. Then she said with a frown, "Tell me again. Why isn't Owen in school?"

Chap told her what he knew.

"But he wants to go to school, right?"

"Oh, yes."

"Well, I hope you can help him with some math, Chap."

As they headed back to the Language Arts Center, De said, with a frown, "How come you're helping that crippled kid anyway?"

Chap shrugged. "I guess because he's a friend like you."

Out of the corner of his eye, Chap saw the smile.

* * *

Three days later, Miss Erin motioned Chap into her office after he and Jean Marie finished their session.

"This is rather complicated, Chap, but I've talked to one of our sponsors about Owen. So far, we haven't enrolled many special needs kids, but our goal is to do so. Maybe Owen can be our first student in a wheelchair. This sponsor is intrigued with the idea of what to do with a kid who reads an encyclopedia but can't do multiplication."

With a pounding heart, Chap listened to the rest of the plan.

In a flurry, the school social worker called Lou Ella and then made a home visit. The next Monday, she brought Lou Ella and Owen to the Academy for a tour. Lou Ella had dressed up for the occasion in snug white jeans and a yellow top knotted at the waist. Owen wore freshly ironed khaki slacks and a green and tan plaid shirt. His carefully combed hair was still damp, but the errant tuft had already sprung up. As they toured the Academy, De silently shadowed them instead of Chap.

The next morning, Chap was standing at the bus stop with Owen, who was smiling more broadly than Chap had ever seen him smile.

"Morning, Miss Dorothea, this is Owen. He'll be going to the Academy with me."

After he helped Owen up the steps, Chap folded his small chair, hefted it onto the bus, and slid it behind Miss Dorothea's seat. As the bus pulled away from the curb, Miss Dorothea began to get Owen's life history. Owen never quit smiling.

Half an hour later, Chap pushed Owen into Miss Sydney's homeroom. De immediately rushed over to meet him.

"So you're Chap's friend?" De said, his arms folded as he looked down at Owen.

"I am," said Owen.

"Well, I'm his friend, too, so I guess we'll both have to be his friends."

With that, they became a duo at school. They were an unlikely pair—three years apart in age but the younger one lots bigger than the older one, one with kinky blonde hair and the other with dark straight hair, one a reader and one a non-reader, one in a wheelchair and the other pushing it, one eager to learn and the other one still professing "I don't do nothin'" even though he was doing a lot.

The diagnostic tests indicated what Chap already knew. Owen was reading at the standardized upper eighth grade level, but his math skills were barely first grade level. De, on the other hand, hadn't yet begun to read even the simplest words although he was close to mastering all the letters of the alphabet and their sounds. His math aptitude was much better. He'd picked up the concept of place value quickly and could count by 1, 2, 3, 4, 5, 10, and 20. He was adding and subtracting two-digit numbers, but he couldn't solve a story problem until someone read it to him.

Within days of Owen's arrival, Miss Sydney and Miss Erin had a small problem on their hands. De and Owen had become the tutors for each other, despite both teachers and older students there to do the job. Owen was helping De sound out words, and De was helping Owen understand place value, using the Cuisenaire rods. They were also working on adding and subtracting. Owen would count out 10 cubes. Then they'd divide them into 1 and 9, 2 and 8, 3 and 7 and so forth.

De would say something like, "Here are 10 cubes. I want only 4, so how many should you take?"

Owen was seeing addition and subtraction, not just memorizing number facts. Shortly after that, Owen started writing his own problems that involved subtraction and addition. The kids really liked to do that, especially when they solved each other's problems.

Neither of the boys had been at the school long enough to be trained to tutor, but that didn't seem to matter. The teachers tried to guide the boys to the qualified student tutors who wore green emblems when they were available to help, but the boys consistently went to each other instead.

At first, Miss Sydney and Miss Erin stayed within earshot of the boys whenever they were in the Math and Language Arts Centers. Later, when they were convinced that the boys were learning and adjusting well to the school, they relaxed. Owen was shown the materials he'd need to use each day for De to begin real reading, and De was given the materials he'd need each day to help Owen go through the Academy's sequential math program.

And so it was as July neared its end.

* * *

July 30ᵗʰ

Dear Tom,

You wrote that it seems that I've turned into a Virginia babysitter. I guess you could say that. I was first "hired" to spend time with Owen. Then, when I started school, I saw him about every evening. I know it's hard for you to believe, but he was desperate to go to school. I can now say "was" since Owen is attending the Academy with me. It's a good thing he's not in a regular school because he can read and comprehend an encyclopedia, but he can barely add and subtract. At the Academy, he is a beaver-sponge. He's doing independent science and social units with others who are his age and older, but he's learning basic math with a tutor, who is De right now.

De is the "no-name" kid I told you about before. A few weeks ago, I gave him the nickname De for his initials— that's "dee" not "duh," by the way. He likes to say, "De is me," and he actually smiles. Mrs. Hunt might object to the grammar. She'd correct it to "De is I," but "De is me" sounds really good from such an angry little kid. He followed me around a lot for a month, proclaiming that he wasn't going to do anything. Now, however, he and Owen are an inseparable pair. This kid helping kid thing is working wonders for those two.

I know that doesn't sound like much, but if you'd ever seen De's angry face and crossed arms, you'd know what a big deal it is to see him being involved in learning at all and taking Owen under his wing.

You know what I keep wondering? I've always liked school for the most part, and you never have much, so if someone like you and most of the guys were in this place, would you like school better, or is the fact I am really enjoying it here all because I already like school? Wow, that's a messed up sentence, but do you get what I mean?

Missing all of you guys, Chap

* * *

The last day of July was miserably hot and steamy. The heat from the sunbaked sidewalks burned through the bottom of Chap's shoes as he pushed the wheelchair toward the apartment complex. Little rivers of sweat trickled down his back, and his hair clung to his forehead. Owen was silent.

In four more days, the Academy would close for the two-week summer break. When Miss Sydney had written the closing date on the homeroom board, Owen had frowned and said loudly, "You can't close now. I just got here!"

Chap wasn't looking forward to the break either, but at least he'd known it was coming. School was the only comfortable part of his new life. The apartment was sterile-looking in all its shades of non-color and cramped besides. Even with the air-conditioner running all the time, it felt stuffy inside. Indiana could also be hot and humid, but the air outside, especially in the woods, had a freshness to it that the air in the city didn't have. The heat radiating from the sidewalks and streets mixed with the fumes of vehicles to make a sort of haze that hung over everything.

Chap couldn't figure out what he'd do to fill the two weeks in the apartment besides spend some time with Owen as he'd done before he'd started going to the Academy. He knew Owen was thinking the same thing. Miss Sydney had told them all that they could plan some lessons to take home, or they could take home nothing during the break, but even the thought of studying at home didn't cheer up either Owen or Chap.

Chap remembered how miserable he'd been in Indiana when he'd "lost" Erica—how what had made him content before he knew her could no longer make him content. He was feeling that way again.

Chapter 7

The next day when Chap was working with Jean Marie in the Math Center, Miss Erin handed him a message. He was to return to homeroom. From then on, he moved in a blur. He called Lori, who was already at the apartment, packing for the trip to Illinois. They'd be leaving as soon as he could get there. Their father was failing.

Within minutes, the social worker appeared, making arrangements for Owen to get home that afternoon and then to and from school for the next couple of days. Chap rushed to find De and Owen to tell them good-bye. Miss Sydney would take care of everything else.

Then he was running to the bus stop—glad that Miss Dorothea was off since he didn't think he could talk to her at that moment.

When he got to the apartment, Lori was fixing sandwiches in the kitchen. She didn't look up, but Chap saw her tear-stained cheeks.

"You'll need clothes for about a week, cool ones for the trip but nicer ones for the hospital. You might want to take some books. . . ."

Her voice choked, and she didn't finish what she was saying, but he knew what she was going to say. They'd be waiting for their father to die.

In silence, they ate some of the sandwiches. Then, while he loaded their suitcases and pillows into the car, she packed the rest of the sandwiches, some fruit, and bottled water into a small cooler. After that, she called to make a motel reservation in Illinois.

As Lori checked the apartment for anything she might've forgotten, Chap called Chicago. When the Andersons' answering machine beeped, Chap said, "Hi, Erica, it's Chap. My father is worse, so Lori and I are leaving right now for Illinois. Maybe I can call you tomorrow."

He left Lori's cell number and hung up.

* * *

Traffic was bumper to bumper as it always seemed to be in the city and even slower on 495 as they headed north. Chap held their father's road atlas in his lap, helping Lori connect with 270 to Fredrick, then 70 to Hagerstown, and finally 68 West that would take them across Maryland's mountainous panhandle. Lori's white-knuckled hands clutched the steering wheel as the miles flew by under their tires. Neither one of them spoke. The sun glared at them as it dropped in the western sky, finally disappearing in a blaze of orange and gold which faded to shades of pink and lavender and then the gray of early evening. They'd stopped once for gas and once at a rest area where they'd eaten the sandwiches she'd packed. It was very late and very dark by the time they got to Morgantown, West Virginia.

As they crossed the border into Pennsylvania on 79 North, Lori suddenly broke into sobs. Grabbing the steering wheel, Chap helped guide the car to the edge of the road.

"I can't go any further. I can't."

"We'll find a place to sleep," Chap said.

"But he can't die alone," she said as tears streamed down her cheeks.

Holding her hand, Chap quietly talked to his sister, telling her that she was doing her best as she'd always done for him and his father—that it was all right to rest now. Their father would want her to rest.

Fifteen minutes later, they pulled into the parking lot of a small motel in the next town. After waking the clerk who dozed, head down on the counter, they got a room and slept in their clothes until dawn.

* * *

That afternoon they stayed at the motel room in Illinois only long enough for quick showers and a change of clothes. Then they drove a few miles on Main Street before turning onto a winding, narrow, flag-lined street that went back to the imposing Veterans' Administration hospital building where the critically ill were cared for.

Holding hands, they climbed the steps, entered through the heavy doors, and turned right down the tiled hallway to room 122. They paused before the partially opened door. Lori's face was white, but her eyes were dry. Chap hoped he looked as ready for whatever was before them as she did.

Their father lay beneath a pale blue blanket, so much smaller than Chap remembered. His lined face was peaceful, his eyes closed. A nurse stood beside the bed, holding his wrist to check his pulse. She looked up as they entered, smiling gently at them.

"I'm glad you've come. He'll know that you're here. Come closer."

They walked up to the bedside, still holding hands. The nurse touched their father's cheek first and then his arm.

"Mr. Smith," she said, leaning close to him, "Lori and Chap are here to see you. Can you open your eyes?"

They stood in the quiet room and waited.

The nurse touched him again. "Open your eyes, Mr. Smith. I know you can."

His lids fluttered and then opened.

"Hi, Dad, it's me, Lori, and Chap. We're here."

His head moved slightly as his eyes focused first on Lori and then on Chap. His hand moved up just a bit. When they reached to hold it, he whispered, "Thank you."

For another minute, he looked at them, whispering "Thank you" two more times. Then he closed his eyes, and his hand relaxed, no longer holding theirs.

As he slept, they talked to Mandy, the nurse who'd been caring for him for about four months.

"How did you know our names?" Lori asked.

She smiled. "I suppose that did seem odd to you. You filled out a family history form when he first came here. You've probably forgotten since you had so much to deal with then. We learn as much as we can about our patients so that we can talk to them, even the ones like your dad who don't respond. Actually, the only things he's said during the past few months are polite things. He used to say to me, 'You're so nice,' but more recently it's been only 'Thank you,' and I haven't heard that for several days."

After the nurse left to check on other patients, Chap and Lori sat on opposite sides of the bed, each holding one of their father's hands while telling him about their lives in Virginia. Only the slight rise and fall of the blue blanket indicated that he was alive.

An hour later, the doctor, a short round-faced man with a ready smile and a heavy accent, told them about their father's failing body. Alzheimer's disease eventually reaches the parts of the brain that control the basic bodily functions which keep a person alive, he explained.

"If I were a doctor on a television drama, I could tell you with certainty that he will pass away in six hours, but I'm just a regular doctor. Your father may live six hours or two days or a week. I encourage you to talk to him as you have been. Tell him about what you remember from when you are kids. Hold his hands. Touch his face. Passing is easier when loved ones are near. I strongly believe that."

The doctor extended his hand to each of them and left the room.

Lori and Chap settled into the chairs again, talking to their father, reading to him, and dozing sometimes, covered with blankets Mandy gave them.

* * *

The next morning, Lori drove back to the motel to shower and eat. She brought Chap some breakfast in a styrofoam container. They turned on a small radio Mandy brought in, finding classical music on one station. They held their father's hands, which no longer held theirs, and talked to him. He didn't open his eyes.

About one o'clock, Lori urged Chap to take a break in the visitors' lounge. As he faced a snack-filled vending machine, trying to get his sleep-deprived brain to make a decision between corn chips and corn curls, a voice behind him said, "Chap?"

His heart pounding, he turned to face Erica.

Chap stared—not moving, not speaking. She was so beautiful—tall and slender, her dark hair pulled back into a braid. She was wearing white slacks and a loose turquoise blouse, which made her blue-green eyes sparkle like sunlight bouncing on ocean swells.

Erica grinned. "Why is this the response I always get from you?" she said.

Chap remembered standing along the wooded country road, facing Erica, who'd just come up behind him on her bicycle, trying to find the words to ask her to help him find his father. He remembered staring at her through the glass in the back door of the big house in Indiana, standing there in his rumpled clothing and bare feet, wondering why she was there, looking so beautiful with her wind-reddened cheeks. He remembered sitting silently in her dad's old pickup truck, searching for the words to make her not hate him.

Then he remembered loving her. She came into his arms as the tears he hadn't shed since leaving Virginia ran down his cheeks. Finally, they sat down on the worn green chairs that lined the dingy cream-colored lounge.

Holding Chap's hands in both of hers, Erica said, "I called Lori when she was at the motel this morning. I asked about driving down. She thought that was a good idea."

Neither spoke for a while. Chap couldn't stop looking at her—afraid that if he glanced away, she'd disappear.

Finally, Erica spoke again. "I saw your father before I came in here. He looks peaceful, Chap. It's good that you're here."

Chap told her what the doctor had said. He and Lori would wait for the end. Their father would not die alone.

"I feel strangely at peace with that. I never told you about the love letters I found in the attic last year. You know, my mom died before I even knew her, and I'd never thought about his relationship with her until I saw the letters. I read only the top one which he'd written shortly before they were married. It was so beautiful. He's lived almost fifteen years without her. Now he'll join her."

Chap's voice broke as he said those last words. Erica held his hands tighter.

* * *

Chap and Erica joined Lori in room 122 for the rest of the afternoon. Lori told her father all about Douglas and about the wedding plans they had. Chap described the Academy. He explained how Owen and De felt like little brothers he needed to look out for—that he liked the feeling of being needed. Erica also talked to the motionless man, telling him how much she cared for Chap and how beautiful it was on First Woods Road.

Around four, Lori went to get a bite to eat. When she returned, Chap and Erica left.

The small family-style restaurant was cozy with old black-and-white photos of local buildings on the walls and large baskets of philodendrons hanging from brackets. Over each booth hung a light with a Tiffany-type, colorful, glass shade. A tall blonde waitress took their orders for salads, fish sandwiches, and cottage-fried potatoes. Chap hadn't realized how little he'd eaten since leaving school two and a half days ago.

Sitting across from each other, their hands touching on the table top, they talked at first about the usual things—the miserably humid weather in Virginia compared to the summer heat of Chicago, relieved by the breezes off Lake Michigan only if one is lucky enough and rich enough to live close to the lake front. He asked about her parents, who were fine, she said.

Then he said bluntly, "You don't limp so much."

She laughed. "You finally noticed."

"I noticed right away, but I was trying to be polite. Is one supposed to comment on a limp at all in this politically correct world?"

Erica laughed—the laugh that he'd fallen in love with so many months ago, the one that had helped fill the long days when he'd been alone with his reticent father in Indiana.

Still smiling, she said, "We don't have to be any kind of correct. We only have to be honest with each other."

She explained that her leg was mostly healed.

"I'll trade this limp for having no pain any day. The doctors say I'll never run marathons or qualify for military service, but I can walk and swim and do about anything else I want to do."

Then Chap told her more about De and Owen and the story about Jean Marie.

Erica laughed. "Are there any more characters at that school?"

"Well, there's Branson. He's ten or eleven. He was my guide the first day—totally bored with the job. When he found out why I'm called Chap, he told me a long tale about his name—about his being conceived in Branson, Missouri, when his older parents, who are archeologists working at the Smithsonian, stayed there before returning from a long tour of the country."

"Unusual name, but he sounds normal enough to me."

"That's what I thought until I learned that his parents aren't older; they're guides at the Smithsonian, not archeologists; he has three younger siblings, and his mother's maiden name is Branson."

Erica laughed again. "How'd you find out all of that?"

"He forgot what he'd told me before, and he gradually let the truth slip out. When I called him on it, he grinned and said, 'Gotcha, didn't I?'"

"It still seems weird that you're telling me all about young kids who are your classmates. How about kids your own age?"

"I play basketball every day with a dozen seniors. They're all normal enough. Three of us will switch our daily activity to running once the weather gets a little cooler."

"What do you mean by 'switch our daily activity'?"

"We have lots of choices for physical activity, just as long as we're active at least thirty minutes a day."

"There aren't regular physical education classes?"

"Not really. The gym teachers work with groups learning fundamentals of lots of different sports, but the goal is to help kids find out what they like to do and will likely continue to do after school. There are adult volunteers who also come in to help. We have a retired high school coach who drops by twice a week to help us improve our game. Besides group activities and sports, we can choose to use the Fitness Center or even dance for some of our physical activity."

"You really like that school, don't you?"

"I do. It's so relaxed without a grade for everything hanging over me. I don't feel like a failure in math like I used to. I just work on a skill or a concept until I get it. More and more, I'm able to figure things out on my own. Jean Marie is still my tutor, so we both go to the Math Center at the same time, but mostly she and three other seniors work on trig with Miss Erin. Actually, any one of them helps me when I get stuck. I like helping little kids and even doing laundry once in a while."

"I wish I could say I like my high school," Erica said, "but I don't know much about it. I had a teacher who came to the house until I could get around easily on crutches. I was in school for regular classes for less than two months. I didn't find any group to fit in with exactly. Mostly, I ate with my chemistry lab partner since we went from that class directly to lunch, but it seems she doesn't want to be friends outside of school. When I called her once this summer, she was too busy to talk, and she never called me back."

Erica shrugged. "Can't say I'm looking forward to school starting after Labor Day."

"I wish I could be there with you—or better yet, you at the Academy with me."

They were quiet for a few minutes as they finished big pieces of chocolate pie with real meringue. The sun was getting low in the summer sky.

"I need to head back to Chicago, Chap. I promised my folks I wouldn't get home too late."

* * *

Erica went into the hospital room to tell Lori good-bye. Then she leaned over to kiss the forehead of the quiet figure beneath the blue blanket.

Chap walked with her to the car.

"I miss you every day, Erica."

Then he kissed her good-bye.

She put her finger to her lips and then to his, repeating what she'd said to him once before at the back door of the house in Indiana, "Don't be lonely."

Chap stood beside the winding street until her car disappeared.

Chapter 8

At dawn on the eighth of August, their father's sixty-second birthday, Chap and Lori stood on the Church Rock high above Wandering River. They watched the ashes float gently away on the early morning breeze—floating down to mingle with the Indiana woods and the river he'd loved.

"I don't suppose you remember when our mother died," Lori said quietly.

Chap shook his head. He had no memory of his mother alive or dead.

"We were all here then—you and I and Dad and Catherine, Julianna, and Marilee. It was a beautiful evening. The woods were all colored in orange, rust, and gold. After her ashes disappeared, we sat on the rock until the sun set. No one wanted to go back to the empty house."

Lori stifled a sob. With tears running down her cheeks, she added, "Part of Dad died then, too. You never got to know him as he was when she was with him. For that, I'm sad for you."

She reached over to take his hand. Neither spoke as the sky turned from shades of pink to orange and gold. When the sun rose above the tree tops, they turned away and walked down the narrow path which descended to First Woods Road.

As they approached the house that was set back a ways from the road, Lori slowed the car and then stopped. For several minutes, they stared at the two-story white house, so quiet in the early morning light. Dark purple petunias and bright yellow marigolds bloomed in the planters which had once contained red geraniums. Three blue boys' bikes of varying sizes lay scattered on the front lawn. White lacy curtains moved gently beyond the screened windows in their father's study. A large gray SUV was parked in front of the one-car garage, which was probably too small to accommodate it.

Lori put the car into gear, and they moved on down First Woods Road. At the wooden bridge, they stopped again. Chap stepped out of the car and walked slowly toward the rail. The great blue heron was standing still in the cattails below, waiting to capture its breakfast. It looked at Chap as if trying to decide whether or not fear of humans would override the desire for a fish. After hesitating a moment, the heron flapped its huge wings slowly to lift its spindly body into the air. Chap watched until it disappeared around the bend of Wandering River.

At the stop sign at the end of First Woods Road, Lori turned left, heading east for the long trip back to Virginia.

Neither one spoke as they drove the familiar eight miles on the county highway to Riverwoods. When they reached the edge of the city, Lori asked, "Do you want to drive around a bit, maybe go by the high school?"

Chap only shook his head. The lump in his throat was huge.

Lori turned onto the state route that skirted the south side of the city. She pulled down the sun visor and donned dark glasses to dim the glare of the morning sun. In less than fifteen minutes, the small city was behind them.

Before leaving Illinois, they'd decided to take several days to get home since it would be their last relaxing days for a long time with Chap in school and Lori and Douglas working, planning a wedding, and hunting for a house. Using their father's atlas, they'd found a route which was pretty much a straight shot from southern Indiana to Washington,

D.C. It was a more scenic, sometimes four-lane and sometimes two-lane highway that wound through lots of small towns in Indiana, Ohio, and West Virginia.

Chap looked out his side window at the alternating woods and fields of corn and soybeans—still growing, still green. Until his father had been taken to the VA hospital in Illinois, Chap had never been out of the state of Indiana, and only occasionally had he been farther from home than Riverwoods. He'd never seen this part of Indiana east of his hometown. As Lori negotiated the gentle hills and curves, the tires hummed, and the sun rose higher.

When Lori slowed down at the edge of the next town, she said, "How about some breakfast? I'm starved. You keep a lookout for some place that might serve food."

At a four-way stop with a business district arrow pointing right, Chap spotted a flower-covered sign for Mary's Café.

"Turn here," he said.

After Lori parked the car, they walked across the street to the café. It was immediately apparent that Mary liked flowers. All the available wall space was covered with painted blossoms of all types and in every shade of lavender, red, pink, blue, yellow, orange, white, and gold. Ivy vines meandered along the tops and bottoms of the walls. Centered on each of the ten tables in the café was a fresh pink carnation in a bud vase.

"Wow," Lori whispered. "Sure hope your testosterone can handle this!"

Chap wrinkled up his nose at her as they took seats at a table under a large window, also decorated with painted flowers. Through small gaps between yellow roses, Chap looked across the street, identifying an insurance office, an antique shop, a five and dime type store, a dentist's office, a pharmacy, and not surprisingly, a flower shop. Shoppers moved along the sidewalk, stopping often to chat.

"Looks like a friendly place, doesn't it?" Lori said.

Chap nodded as an ancient, white-haired waitress in a pink dress, lacy apron, and clunky orthopedic shoes shuffled to the table, coffee pot in hand.

"What's your preference?" she said, instead of the more usual, "Are you ready to order?"

"My preference is pancakes and scrambled eggs with a cup of coffee," Lori said.

Chap ordered the same thing with a large orange juice instead of coffee.

After the waitress left the table and moved slowly toward the kitchen, Lori said abruptly, "Have you ever wondered why our sisters left home?"

Chap shrugged. "Not really. I was so little I just accepted things as they were."

He looked down at his hands and then added, "When I think back, I see all four of you as a blur. You looked so much alike—all about the same size with short, dark, curly hair. I never really got to know Catherine and Julianna as individuals, so I didn't miss them much when they left. I remember Marilee a little better, but I was still pretty young when she left."

"You were what—seven?"

"Seven and a half."

"And I was not quite sixteen."

They were silent as the waitress placed the golden pancakes and eggs before them. Then she surveyed the table and said not the usual "Is there anything else?" but "Let's see. What did I forget?"

Suppressing a smile, Lori said, "It looks fine to me."

The waitress shrugged, turned, and shuffled off.

When her plate was about half empty, Lori laid down her fork and said, "Our mother was a genius at organization. She had to be with a new baby on the scene every other fall for years and frequent moves to various army bases. She learned right away to delegate tasks. When I was three, I remember being bathed and dressed by Catherine, who was just nine years old, and Julianna, at age seven, helped Marilee. Long before we started school, we all learned to make our own beds, put away our clean clothes, and set and clear the table.

"When she died, Dad was suddenly faced with running a household with daughters ages ten, twelve, fourteen, and sixteen and you just a toddler. Even I, at age ten, felt us all falling apart until suddenly his military training grabbed hold, and we became a well-run barracks. Mother had kept things running smoothly with gentle prods and praise. Our father did it with a loud voice and stern looks—especially toward Catherine and Julianna, who were in high school."

Lori paused and resumed eating.

"You know," Chap said, "what I do remember is the mealtime reports. Each of you girls had to tell about something that had happened during the day, or you had to answer questions he posed. He started asking me when I was in kindergarten."

Lori laughed. "Oh, I remember that!"

"Yeah, me, too. I was petrified when he demanded to know what I'd learned that day, and all of you were staring at me, so I told him that I'd learned not to pee in the sand box, which some kid had done. I saw the playground monitor haul him into the principal's office."

"Oh, Chap, I knew you were in trouble the minute the words were out of your mouth. He thought you were being a smart aleck."

"Was that the first time you shoved me up the stairs to the attic?"

"I don't think so. You got your mouth washed out with soap that evening. It was later that fall that you did something else to set him off, and I had you hide in the attic."

"I just remember running up there sometimes until he quit yelling."

Chap paused. Then he added, "But he never hit any of us when we were kids, did he?"

Lori shook her head as tears welled up in her eyes.

"No, but he was very strict. Catherine, as the oldest, felt the most pressure. He expected good grades and unquestioned obedience. He restricted her social life to one date night a week with an eleven o'clock curfew. When Catherine met John, she saw a way out. He was twenty-three, good looking, and ready to see the world. They eloped three weeks after she graduated from high school and headed west. Dad was furious. We didn't hear much from her for a couple of years, but after Peggy was born, she wrote more often. For a while, Dad read the letters at the dinner time. Then he quit doing that. I guess we know why now."

Lori idly began to stir her coffee. Finally, she picked up the cup and drained it. After looking at her watch, she reached for the check. As she laid down a very big tip, she whispered, "A memorable breakfast in a flower garden with such an interesting waitress deserves something special."

A few minutes later, they were again heading east toward Virginia. Lori picked up the story of their sisters.

"Then Julianna left for college as expected. She'd gotten a scholarship to art school in Missouri.

"Marilee was the problem child. She never followed the routines without being pushed. She hated school and did just enough to avoid getting grounded. She really knew how to push Dad's buttons. Frankly, it was almost a relief when she took the five hundred dollars from his desk and disappeared. You know about her infrequent postcards. She's somewhere in California, still trying to get into movies or television, she says."

Lori was quiet again as she negotiated around an old green farm tractor pulling a huge flat-bed wagon piled high with bales of hay.

As she slowed for another town, she said, "Let's take a break. I see a sign for a yard sale."

Twenty minutes later, they were back in the car. Chap had found a ceramic cat for Owen and Lou Ella—not a purple and blue reclining cat like Nelson Nelson had smashed but a regal Siamese with bright blue eyes, sitting tall with its tail curled around its front paws. He also bought six polo shirts like the ones he usually wore to school. Some guy his size had apparently bought every color offered since Chap had a choice of nine colors, but he passed on pink, dark purple, and gold. He also found several books for both Owen and De and a bright pink bandana that Jean Marie might wear around her neck to brighten up her black wardrobe.

They moseyed along the rest of the day, touring a historic court house in Indiana and taking a walk in a nature reserve. That night they stayed in a tiny cabin at a mom-and-pop motel in central Ohio.

After a leisurely breakfast the next morning, they headed east again, but as the day progressed, their stops became less frequent. At Clarksburg, West Virginia, the road became all two-lane, winding up and down the mountains, not at all the straight line shown in the atlas. They were in Maryland for a short time as the highway crossed the triangular southern tip of the panhandle. The deciduous forests were lovely, still lush and green, leading Chap to wonder if he might be seeing places, hidden in the dense foliage, where no man had ever trod.

When the sun began to set, they pulled into the parking lot of a rundown motel in bad need of a coat of paint, the only motel they'd seen for over an hour. Lori turned off the engine, but she didn't get out of the car.

Suddenly, she said exactly what Chap was thinking. "Let's go on home."

Chap smiled as they pulled back onto the narrow highway.

The traffic thinned as darkness crept in. Carefully, Lori navigated the rise and fall, twists and turns of the highway that was nearly deserted by midnight. Near Winchester, Virginia, the road was once again a wide four-lane. Then 495, which encircled the Washington area, seemed eerie in the wee morning hours without the usual jam of cars and trucks. At 2:30, they carried only their pillows and suitcases into the apartment and fell into bed.

Chapter 9

The bright morning sun, peeking through the slats of the window blind, fell across Chap's eyes. He turned his head to escape it, but the smell of coffee and bacon further intruded into his sleep. Stretching, he threw back the top sheet and walked to the door of his room.

Lori was standing at the stove, turning the sizzling bacon with one hand and sipping coffee from the mug she held in the other.

"Well, lazy bones, I see that you've decided to join the living. Breakfast in ten, so why don't you take a fast shower so that you'll be presentable."

"Let me guess. Douglas is coming."

"That he is. You may not believe this, but he's missed me."

"Wait until he knows you like I do."

"Hey," she said, wrinkling up her nose at him, "go get decent, or I'll burn your bacon!"

"That's extortion. You know bacon is my favorite food!"

With mock seriousness, she pointed at his room and raised her eyebrows.

Laughing, Chap ducked into the tiny shower stall in his bathroom and turned on the water.

It felt good to be home again. He'd made fun of Lori when she'd said that very thing at 2:30 in the morning as they pulled into the parking lot.

"It's pathetic," he'd said, "to call this colorless little apartment home, but I'm glad to be here, too."

After stepping out of the shower, Chap toweled himself dry and pulled on clean khaki shorts and a white polo. He was thinking about home. For the past several months, that word had meant only the big house in Indiana. But yesterday, home had become this cramped apartment where he was with Lori. Soon home would be wherever he, Lori, and Douglas would be living—at least he hoped so.

With that thought, he opened his bedroom door. Douglas was standing behind Lori, nuzzling her neck as she stirred the scrambled eggs.

"Morning," Chap said.

Douglas jumped back from Lori as if caught in a criminal act.

Chap grinned. "For heavens' sake, Douglas, it's not like I'm an older brother, holding a shotgun on the man who might violate his little sister."

"Funny, Chap," he said, his blue eyes squinting and his tone sarcastic.

Turning to Lori, he said, "Are you sure he's your brother?"

"Sorry, but I'm sure."

"Sure, sure, or just maybe sure? You know he's tall and you're—well, you know—not tall."

"Nice wording—to avoid the word *short*."

"Besides that, he has straight hair, not curly, and his eyes are kinda. . . ." He leaned toward Chap and peered at his face. "Kinda grayish, not dark like yours."

"I know, but he's my brother."

"So we have to keep him?"

"We do."

Walking toward the dinette table, Chap said, "Are you two comedians about done? I don't know about you, but I'm hungry."

He was grinning as he sat down. It did feel good to be home.

* * *

The last days of the summer break flew by. Lori and Douglas included both Chap and Owen on a trip into D.C. to tour the monuments, which Owen had never seen. That fact surprised Chap since Owen had lived in the area all his life and, at the same time, seemed incredibly sad because it indicated that Owen's life had been limited to the four wall of his apartment for all of his ten years.

The four of them had such a good time that they went back the next morning to spend a whole day at the Smithsonian.

Then twice Chap went with Owen and Lou Ella to therapy that Owen had started after being evaluated by a pediatric specialist whose children attended the Academy. The diagnosis: Owen's inability to walk more than a very short distance was the result of not walking. His leg muscles had atrophied since he'd been sitting for most of his life—Lou Ella's solution to his early problems of learning how to walk at all. Owen had thought he couldn't walk, so he'd never tried much to do so. Without regular doctor visits during his first five years, no one had contradicted that idea. When he'd first entered public school, the disability was simply accepted by the faculty and staff there as well as the clinic doctor who gave him the required immunizations.

Owen was ecstatic. "The doctor says that if I work hard, I can learn to walk. My back will always be a little crooked, but I'll be able to really walk!"

Chap forced a smile. Because of the jumble of his angry emotions, he was having trouble concentrating on the chess game they were playing. A baby boy had been born with a disability made worse by an absent mother and a grandmother who'd simply decided to plunk her less-than-perfect grandson into a tiny wheelchair. But nowhere in Owen's gentle soul was there room for anger at having been cheated out of being a regular kid.

"I'm going to do special exercises at school, too," Owen said as he moved a pawn. "The doctor will show Mr. Joe what I need to do. One of these days, I'll ditch this chair. Don't tell De or Miss Sydney. I want to surprise them when I show up without it."

Owen grinned as he so often did since entering the Academy.

"You know, Chap. You must be my guardian angel. First, you get me into a school, and now because of that, I'll be strong enough to walk."

"What will I become when you no longer need me to push you around?" Chap said, frowning as he tried to look very serious.

"Oh, I'll always need you to be my friend," Owen said, looking alarmed that Chap's feelings might be hurt.

"Got you!" Chap said with a grin. "I'm kidding."

"You continue to be one of those things I can't say!" Owen replied, his brow furrowed as he moved another chess piece and put Chap's king in jeopardy.

* * *

August finally melted away, and September began. Chap waited to feel the hint of fall in the air, but it didn't come. September in Virginia wasn't much different from August, at least as far as the weather was concerned.

Chap was well established in his routine at the Academy. He started with a couple of hours each morning in the Language Arts Center, working now with two other seniors, Shannon and Keya, on the literature-history class. They'd decided to read independently but to meet daily to discuss what they'd read. They'd also decided to do a project together, each contributing different elements to the basic topic of what kind of influence the written word had had on the slavery issue before the Civil War.

His math was coming along well. He had only one more weak area to master before he'd start a condensed algebra class to review what he'd worked on—not always successfully—the previous year at Riverwoods High. After that, it was on to geometry and advanced algebra. He was passing the on-line music class—actually enjoying it—and acing the science units. He was even speaking Spanish twice a week with a volunteer, an elderly retired teacher who was born in Peru.

He was also helping three young readers, including De, with oral reading and flash cards for sight words. After De had mastered phonics in the YAK program in record time, he'd been unstoppable in learning to read. De was rapidly becoming an Academy success story.

His foster mom, Miss April, had come to meet Chap and Owen in late August. She was a round-faced, light-skinned black lady with a short Afro.

"I just had to meet the two guys De talks about all the time."

Extending her hand to Chap, she added, "You must be the name giver. It was pure genius to think of 'De.' He says your name is like his, an 'acrobat.'"

She laughed, a soft chuckle that bubbled up from deep inside. Chap and Owen also laughed.

"He means *acronym*," Owen said, and then he told the story about Chap's four names.

"You are a very special young man, Owen. We don't think De has ever had a friend like you before. He is so proud when he helps you. He claims that you need him."

She smiled and continued, "When Mr. Allan and I remind him that you're also helping him, he admits that you do help him read, but then he repeats how he helps you with math and walking."

As she talked, Chap wondered if Owen had ever had a friend like De.

"Anyway, I wanted to meet you gentlemen. Thanks so much for helping such an angry kid get out of his shell and smile. I'm sure I'll be seeing a lot of you both."

Soon after that, Lou Ella began to allow Owen to spend time with De's family whenever he was invited over. One afternoon, as Owen and Chap headed to the apartment complex from the bus stop, Owen was telling about his latest visit. He said, "They're the first real family I've ever met—you know, two parents and some kids, even if they look funny."

"What do you mean 'funny'?"

"Well, Miss April is kinda black and Mr. Allan has red hair. He's Irish."

"How do you know that?"

"O'Neill is an Irish name, Chap. Anyway, pictures in the living room of their two older sons—they're in college now—show one looking mostly like Miss April and one mostly like Mr. Allan. Then there's Leeza, the four-year-old black foster daughter they recently adopted, and now De, who is white with fuzzy blonde hair and blue eyes."

Owen added with a grin, "Wonder what color their next foster kid will be?"

Chap laughed. All in all, school was going well.

At home, Lori was all consumed with wedding plans even though she wanted a simple service and a buffet dinner immediately afterwards. Still, there were decisions about flowers and music and food and the cake. Only Chap had been allowed to see her dress—a beautifully simple ivory gown with a snug bodice, a flowing mid-calf length skirt, and long fitted sleeves.

"No bows, no bustle, no plunging neckline, no pearls or rhinestones, no train, no veil," she'd said to the astonished clerk at the first bridal shop they'd gone to in August.

Finding elegantly simple had turned out to be harder than Lori had thought, but her choice seemed perfect to Chap when he accompanied her to the fitting in late September.

Douglas was at the apartment almost every evening for supper, often cooking it himself. Soon he and Chap were able to talk easily as Chap helped. For most of his life, Chap had weighed his words carefully, often letting the chance to speak slip by while he tried to figure out what to say. He'd always talked to Lori easily, but it was months after he'd first met Erica before he was able to speak to her and then only after his words had first hurt her feelings. Now he could count Douglas among those with whom he felt comfortable. Any resentment he'd felt toward his almost brother-in-law for being the main reason they'd left Indiana was gone.

Actually, they had quite a bit in common, and there were all sorts of topics for them to talk about. They were tall guys. Douglas at over six feet and Chap at six both dwarfed Lori, who was five foot two. They were only sons with sisters—Douglas with two younger ones and Chap with four older ones. Both had lost their mothers when they were young. Chap had no memories of his mother, who'd collapsed the fall before he was two and died from an uncorrectable heart defect. Douglas's mother had been killed in a freak accident when a violent straight-line wind toppled an old tree which crushed her car as she was returning home from the grocery store. Douglas was not quite seven. He and his dad were alone for almost three years before his dad met his step-mom, the school nurse, when Douglas fell off the jungle gym on the playground one day.

As they were doing dishes one evening, Douglas said, "I got a great new mom—no evil step-mother for me—and then two little sisters shortly after that. I'm thirteen years older than Jackie and fifteen years older than Ashley."

"I think it was easier for me," Chap said. "I never knew what I'd lost, even when my three oldest sisters left before I was eight. Lori just stepped into the mother role when she was the only one left at home. My dad was different then, actually part of our lives for quite a few years. Then, when he started to withdraw, Lori was always there."

Douglas looked over at Lori, who was all involved in a mystery novel, and said, "Well, I think we'll always agree on one thing, Chap. She's great!"

"You think so? Wait until she bosses you around. 'Take out the trash, Douglas. Pay the electric bill, Douglas. Put the cap back on the toothpaste, Douglas.'"

A throw pillow sailed into the kitchen from the living room. Apparently, Lori wasn't as engrossed in her book as they'd thought. Both guys grinned.

"By the way, have you always been called Douglas?"

"No, it was Dougie until I was about thirteen. By then, I was getting some grief from a group of guys with names like Brandon, Chuck, and Mike. They were putting lots of emphasis on the last syllable, if you know what I mean, so I entered high school as Douglas. I refused to answer to Doug or Dougie even at home."

Chap didn't say anything. He just kept drying dishes.

"You have an opinion here?"

"Well, when I was called Charles Henry at home, I knew I was in trouble. If the Anthony Peter was added, I was looking at a life sentence."

Douglas laughed.

"When I call you Douglas, I almost feel like I'm reprimanding you," Chap said with a shrug.

"So you want to call me Doug?"

"If that's okay with you."

"Anything for an almost brother-in-law. We have to stay united as minority males in our families dominated by females."

Another throw pillow flew into the kitchen. Both grinned as Doug punched Chap in the shoulder. Within a week, Lori was also calling her fiancé Doug.

As the rest of September passed and October began, they enjoyed their quiet evenings together—sometimes reading, sometimes watching television, sometimes playing games like Scrabble or dominoes or Bananagrams, sometimes walking to the ice cream shop nearby or a movie theater. Life was again settled and comfortable.

Chapter 10

Monday, October 14, started as an ordinary day. The wedding was just one month away, but instead of becoming more tense and anxious, Lori seemed to relax.

"It's all planned. It will be what it will be," she said with a shrug.

Moving day was set for October 30. The year's lease for a house had been signed. After not finding a home they wished to buy, Lori and Doug had found a three-bedroom ranch to rent in a neighborhood less than fifteen minutes from their jobs. Lori wanted a house with some grass and flowers of their own, not a condo with maybe just a postage-sized yard or no yard at all. Before signing the lease, they'd visited the house twice, trying to get a view of the neighborhood. The grade-school-aged kids getting off the bus on a Thursday afternoon indicated that it was a mixed neighborhood since the kids seemed to be of every size, shape, and color. A visit there on the following Saturday afternoon indicated that the neighborhood was also a mixed-age one since those out with their dogs included a white-haired Indian woman in a red and gold sari who was walking a small black terrier and a teen-aged boy who was "walking" his Great Dane by riding his bike as the huge caramel-colored dog trotted along beside him.

Chap's bus ride would increase to forty-five minutes with a transfer from a new bus to Miss Dorothea's, but he felt the change, which would shorten the commute for Lori and Doug, was worth it.

The only downside to the whole move was leaving Owen. Chap could hardly look him in the eye when he asked about the house. Owen had never lived in a house, never played in his own yard, never enjoyed neighbors who didn't move away after a short time.

That mid-October morning, Owen walked to the bus stop, pushing his empty wheelchair. He was getting stronger every week. His goal was to get himself to and from the bus stop with his chair but without Chap's help in just two more weeks and to get himself to school without his chair by Christmas.

When they got close to the Academy, Owen sat down in his chair and wheeled himself inside. After homeroom, Chap and Owen parted. First, Chap helped his young tutees with sight words containing *gh*. Then, while doing a load of laundry, he worked on an essay about how Jim Crow laws had kept the black population enslaved in the South long after the 13th Amendment was passed. In the Math Center, he tackled a page of binomials, asking Jean Marie for help only twice. Before lunch, he ran through a neighborhood park with three other guys. That afternoon, he worked on science, Spanish, and music. It was an ordinary day at the Academy.

That warm fall evening was also ordinary. He and Doug fixed a tuna casserole and a fruit salad for supper. After the dishes were cleared, the three of them sat down at the table to play Bananagrams.

As they silently moved their tiles around to make crosswords, the television next door blared as usual with an episode of *Golden Girls*. A cool breeze with a hint of Lou Ella's cigarette smoke came in through the open patio door.

Suddenly, all three of them started when the front door of the Barskys' apartment slammed shut. Not moving, they listened for voices through the thin apartment walls, but when the only sound continued to be the television, they went back to concentrating on their tiles.

Chap said, "Peel," after he moved his last two tiles to make another word.

Lori and Doug groaned as each of them drew a new tile.

Quickly, Chap again said, "Peel" after he placed the *x* he'd drawn beside an *a* to make *ax* and then "Peel" once more as he added an *e* to make *axe.*

The groans from his competitors got louder as Chap grinned.

All at once, their hands froze on their tiles. Nelson Nelson's voice was low at first, and then, rapidly rising, it drowned out the sound of the television.

"Get that kid out of here," he bellowed.

Then there was pandemonium. Crashing sounds came from the Barskys' apartment as something was smashed again and again against the wall.

Lou Ella screamed, "Stop! Stop!"

As Lori raced to the bar in the kitchen to grab her phone, Doug sprinted toward the patio door with Chap right behind him. They vaulted over the low railings separating the patios. Doug flung the Barskys' patio screen door wide open.

Nelson Nelson was swinging a baseball bat wildly, shattering a lamp, denting Owen's wheel chair, putting another hole in the wall near the dinette table. His face was contorted in anger, his gray beard stubble in contrast with his red cheeks. His thin dirty white tee shirt was partially pulled out of his ragged jeans.

Chap froze as he stared down at Lou Ella, who lay on the floor near the patio door, not moving. Her right leg was twisted unnaturally, and blood oozed from a gaping gash on her scalp, turning her dark red hair even darker and soaking into the beige carpet around her head.

Owen was cowering beneath the dinette table—his right arm hanging uselessly, his face stark white. "She's dead," he sobbed.

With his heart pounding in his ears, Chap dropped to the floor beside Lou Ella. Gently, he put his hand on her neck. When he felt a pulse, he said, "She's alive."

Doug was inching slowly toward Nelson Nelson, his arms held out from his sides, his palms up in an unthreatening pose. Chap rose and followed, mimicking Doug's pose.

"Put the bat down, man. Put the bat down," Doug said evenly and quietly.

Still swinging the bat, Nelson Nelson stepped back, shattering first the ceramic Siamese cat and then the flimsy coffee table.

"Put the bat down," Doug repeated, a bit louder this time. "You don't want to hurt anyone else."

Glaring at them with unfocused, bloodshot eyes, he growled, "The bitch won't get rid of that bastard kid."

Lightning quick, he smashed the bat down onto the wheelchair three more times. Doug and Chap jumped back. Then, suddenly, Nelson Nelson turned and staggered from the apartment, slamming the door behind him.

"I need to see where he goes. Stay here," Doug commanded.

Chap stood in shocked silence as Doug left the apartment. Behind him, tiny soft whimpers came from Owen.

Moments later, Doug returned to the apartment. "He's driving a dark beat-up Ford, I think, with a light hood—maybe primer paint. I didn't get too close to him. I saw only 381 on the license plate."

Then Doug stared at the destruction all around him as if seeing it for the first time. When his eyes rested on the still form of Lou Ella, he said, "Oh, God, what has he done?"

Lori dashed in from the patio. As the color drained from her face, she swayed. Doug moved quickly to place his arm around her.

"The police are on their way," she said as tears streamed down her cheeks.

Quickly recovering her composure, she brushed away the tears and grabbed a blanket from the back of the couch. Kneeling beside Lou Ella, she tucked it tightly around the unmoving woman. Then she ran to the bathroom, returning with a damp towel which she gently pressed against the gash on Lou Ella's scalp.

Carefully, Chap helped Owen out from under the table. A large flaming-red spot on Owen's cheek was already beginning to darken. He was holding his right arm tightly with his left hand. With a sob, he dropped to the floor beside his grandmother. Chap knelt down beside him, holding Owen as he cried.

Thus they stayed—three kneeling beside Lou Ella and Doug standing—until loud knocking and yells of "Police" broke the stillness. When Doug flung the door open, two officers rushed in with their hands resting on their holstered weapons.

"He's gone," Doug said quietly.

* * *

October 14

Dear Erica,

We're sitting in the emergency room at St. Anne's. Doug is holding Lori, who is still as pale as a ghost. I'm sure I'll call you tomorrow and tell you all that I'm going to write, but I need to "talk" to you right now. We aren't hurt, but Owen and Lou Ella are.

Remember Nelson Nelson? I told you about him before—the man Owen finally admitted was yelling in their apartment. He came tonight with a baseball bat and hurt Lou Ella and Owen. When we first heard the yells from Nelson Nelson and Lou Ella, Doug and I rushed to their apartment. We got in through the open patio door. But it was too late. Doug tried to get him to put down the bat, but he kept swinging it. He made holes in the walls, broke a lamp and other glass things, smashed the coffee table, and pretty much destroyed Owen's wheelchair.

Lori called the police—so had others in the apartment complex—and though it felt like a long time, the first two officers got there in less than ten minutes. Then the apartment was filled with more police, the EMTs who worked on Lou Ella and Owen before taking them away in an ambulance, and several crime scene ladies who took many pictures.

A detective named Jarvek talked to the three of us for quite a while, first wanting to know about our relationship with the Barskys and then asking lots and lots of questions about exactly what we saw and what we know about Nelson Nelson. We're supposed to go down to the local station tomorrow to make formal statements. Finally, the police vacated the apartment, leaving only the yellow crime scene tape.

Then we drove here. Since we aren't family, we didn't know if we'd be able to find out anything, but Owen had been asking for us, so we've gotten some information.

The lower bone is broken in Owen's right arm, and he has a nasty bruise on his face. He'll be kept at least overnight for observation after his arm is set. He's in x-ray right now. Lou Ella is more badly hurt. Her right leg is shattered, and the doctors are concerned about the head injury. Nelson Nelson apparently hit her with the bat at least twice. She hasn't regained consciousness, so they're trying to get her stable before she goes into surgery to get the leg bone back together.

Since Owen has no idea where his mother is—he hasn't seen her in months—and has never even met his father, a woman from Children's Services is here with us. I told her about the Academy, which she is already familiar with since she's placed children in the past with Miss April and Mr. Allan. I also told her about De and Owen being so close. Maybe something good can come out of this if Owen is placed with De. I'm afraid to hope.

I'm wondering if this is making any sense. It's about 1 a.m. now. Please excuse the notebook paper. For some crazy reason, I grabbed my school backpack when we left—like I could concentrate on studying? Anyway, as soon as we know that Owen is settled in a room, we'll leave.

I've never seen evil like this. I don't think it's really sunk it yet—the idea that Nelson Nelson could've killed them both. Owen is such a gentle little soul. Why would anyone ever hurt a child like that? Or Lou Ella, for that matter?

I've got to go. Owen is back from x-ray now. He's asked for me to sit with him while the cast is put on.

Thanks for listening.

I love you so much, Chap

* * *

In the wee hours of the morning, the apartment was eerily quiet with lots of lights on and the tiles of the unfinished Bananagrams crosswords still lying on the table. Lori stood in the doorway as if waiting for someone to come greet them. Then she laid her jacket and purse on a living room chair and started toward the table.

When she reached for the yellow banana-shaped bag for the tiles, Doug said, "Not now, honey. Just go to bed."

Lori shoulders sagged, and she leaned on the table for support. Doug took her in his arms.

Still standing near the apartment door, Chap said quietly, "Doug, can you stay with us? I don't think either one of us wants you to leave."

"But where will he—"

Chap held up his hand to silence Lori. "He'll sleep with you. Good-night."

With that, Chap turned and entered his bedroom, closing the door gently.

* * *

About ten the next morning, Doug, Chap, and Lori entered the Academy. At the Command Center, Chap said, "Miss Celia, I'm not coming to school today, but we need to see Miss Sydney and Miss Erin. Owen won't be here either."

After Miss Celia gave Lori and Doug visitor badges, they followed Chap to the Language Arts Center. Miss Sydney was walking from group to group. A green tag around her neck indicated that she was available to help anyone.

As Chap approached, she grinned and said quietly, "Slept in, huh?"

Then her smile faded when she saw Lori and Doug.

"Something's wrong," she said, making it a statement, not a question. "Where's Owen?"

"Can we go into the office?" Chap said, his voice breaking.

As Doug briefly described the events at the Barskys' apartment, Miss Sydney wept. After wiping her eyes, she and Chap went to speak to Shannon and Keya. When Chap explained that he'd be gone for a day or two, the girls decided to work on something else until he returned to join their group. Then Miss Sydney asked an aide to go find Miss Erin and the social worker.

In short order, several decisions were made. The social worker would contact the woman from Children's Services who'd been at the hospital the night before. Soon De and Miss April joined the group in Miss Sydney's office. De was told the truth. Owen was hurt, but he'd recover in time. Miss April already knew what her role would likely be in helping him get well.

Before leaving the Academy, Chap tracked down Jean Marie in the gym to tell her he'd be gone for a while. Then, in the Science Center, he found Charlie, who agreed to do Chap's share of the laundry as well as his own until Chap returned.

Fifteen minutes later, Lori, Doug, and Chap left the Academy. As they drove to the police station, Lori said, "They certainly know how to get things done at that school. Do you suppose Owen will be placed with the O'Neills right away? I thought things like that took a long time to go through the system."

"I get the feeling that some people associated with the Academy have influence and know how to get past red tape. Didn't it take less than a week to get Owen enrolled at the Academy to begin with?" Doug said.

Chap listened to the talk, hoping beyond hope that Owen would go "home" from the hospital to the O'Neills. Maybe the color of their next foster kid would be white with straight brown hair, a rakish cowlick, and a white face marred temporarily with a huge ugly bruise.

At the police station, they were ushered into Detective Jarvek's office, a small room with lots of file cabinets and a desk buried beneath files and all kinds of paper. Lori and Chap sat down in the only two extra chairs while Doug stood behind Lori, his hands resting on her shoulders.

Though Chap had talked to Detective Jarvek at the Barskys' apartment less than twenty-four hours earlier, Chap felt as if he were seeing him for the first time. Though the muscular gray-haired detective had likely been wearing a suit and tie on the job for years, it seemed to Chap that he'd have been more comfortable on a practice field, dressed in sweats and coaching a football team. Chap stared at the detective's huge hands, which were folded on his desk top as he leaned forward to ask questions. Chap figured that if those hands nabbed you, you were caught for sure.

In answer to Doug's first question—had Nelson Nelson been caught—the detective said, "Not yet, but it won't take long. He's probably in his car somewhere, sleeping it off. Patrol officers all around the D.C. area are looking for that car you described."

"What'll happen when he's arrested?" Lori asked.

"Well, with you three very credible eye witnesses and the fact he was breaking his parole by even being at the apartment, he'll never see light of day again, in my opinion. For God's sake, the man brutally attacked a child and an elderly woman with a bat! Even I don't see that too often."

Chap stared at the detective's clenched hands, the knuckles white.

"Will we have to testify?" Doug asked.

"That depends." The detective shrugged. "If he pleads guilty, maybe just at a sentencing hearing. We'll know more about that later. Right now, let's just get your statements on the record."

Lori stayed with Detective Jarvek. Chap and Doug were escorted to separate rooms with two other detectives. About half an hour later, all three were finished.

As Detective Jarvek shook their hands, he said, "You saved their lives. Not everybody looks out for their neighbors in this day and age. It's a pleasure knowing you all."

* * *

After the waitress placed their lunches on the table at a nearby café, Chap stared at his cheeseburger. Lori and Doug continued to talk about their statements to the police.

Finally, Lori said, "Chap, aren't you hungry?"

"Oh, yes, I guess I am."

"Something's bothering you," she said.

Chap looked into the faces of the sister, with whom he'd always been able to talk, and Doug, who already felt like the brother he'd never had.

Instead of saying, "No problem, just tired," he said, "I could've kept them from getting hurt."

"No, you couldn't. You and Doug got there as fast as you could."

"I don't mean last night. I mean last summer."

Then he told about Owen begging Chap not to mess it up for Lou Ella.

"I knew then that Nelson Nelson wasn't allowed to be there, but I never told anyone."

"Oh, Chap, this isn't on your shoulders," Lori said. "Think about it. The parole board thought Nelson Nelson was rehabilitated. Lou Ella wanted the man she'd once loved back, and she let him into the apartment. Owen wanted his grandma to be happy, so he ignored his fears. I didn't call the police when we heard him yelling those two times."

Lori was silent awhile. Then she added, "See what I mean? This isn't on you. What happened is no one's fault except for that awful man."

Frowning, Chap thought about what his sister had said. Then he picked up his cheeseburger and said, "I get it."

* * *

When they walked into the hospital room that afternoon, Owen's face lit up. His smile was crooked because of the swelling on one side of his face.

"Don't I look colorful?" he said, removing the ice bag from his cheek. "That's what the nurses are telling me. I've got the most beautiful shades of purple they've seen in a long time."

Chap grinned. Leave it up to Owen to be cheerful, even in a hospital bed.

"And look at all of this," he said, pointing at a small bouquet of yellow daisies, a huge chocolate chip cookie with "We Miss You" written in blue icing, and a couple of cards. "The flowers are from Miss Sydney and the cookie from Miss April and De, and the cards were signed by a whole bunch of kids. I don't even know them all!"

"How long are you going to stay here?" Lori asked.

Owen's smile faded. He shrugged.

"I'm sorry, Owen. I didn't mean to make you sad."

Tears welled up in his eyes. "I can't go home. Lou Ella's bad hurt— way worse than me. What's going to happen to me?"

Lori sat down on the edge of the bed and held his hand.

"Lots of people care about what happens to you. Look at what you have here already. Someone will help you. You aren't alone. We'll come see you often when you get settled somewhere else. I promise."

Doug and Chap nodded.

Owen snuggled back on his pillows. His face relaxed a bit.

"You need rest. We'll see you later," Doug said.

Owen waved his good arm as they left the room.

At the nurse's station, they met the social worker, Ms. Alexander, who'd been there last night. She briefly described Lou Ella's condition. The surgery on her leg had been completed, but she was still unconscious in the ICU.

"Owen won't be living with his grandmother for a long time—if ever again. I'll be telling Owen that today. It's important that you know that since you seem to be the people he counts on the most."

"Can he go live with O'Neills?" Chap blurted out.

She smiled. "If you pray at all, that's what I'd pray for."

* * *

Journal Entry #7 - October 21

I know it hasn't been too long since I last wrote, but a lot has happened that I want to tell you about. I told you that Lori and I will be moving in just about a week to a real house and that I was concerned about leaving Owen, who has become almost like a little brother. Well, a very bad man has changed everything.

A week ago, that man, who used to be married to his grandma, attacked both Owen and Lou Ella with a bat. Doug and I were able to stop him from hurting them even more. Even so, Lou Ella was badly beaten. Her shattered leg will heal, but the head injury will likely cause her to be totally disabled for the rest of her life.

That fact has put Owen, who has a broken arm and a bruised face, into the foster care system since no one knows where his mother is. As awful as it sounds, her absence has turned out to be a good thing. If she were around, Owen might have to live with her, or it could take time to prove that she isn't a fit mother. Owen hardly knows her, it seems, since she is rarely with him. I've seen her only twice in almost five months—and then only when she was asleep on the couch in their apartment.

Someone at the Academy must have major pull because Owen went directly from the hospital to live with De's foster parents. It turned out that the woman from Children's Services who was called to the hospital the night Owen was hurt is the case worker for the O'Neills. Once she knew that Owen was also going to the Academy, the rest fell into place in a hurry.

We are leaving Owen in good hands. I will continue to see him and De at the Academy. Sometimes bad things in life turn out good.

Nelson Nelson was apprehended a few days ago. He's in jail with no bond. We're hoping he'll plead guilty so that the three of us and Owen don't have to be involved in a trial. Detective Jarvek thinks he'll spend the rest of his life behind bars.

Right now, we're trying to concentrate on getting packed up to move on the 30th. Then we'll have about two weeks to get organized before the wedding. No stress here.

Thanks for the ear, Mrs. Hunt.

Chapter 11

Chap walked into the living room, now free of moving boxes, and tossed his jacket onto the back of the couch. Fall had finally come to Virginia. It was Thursday, November 12—two days and counting before the wedding on Saturday.

Walking toward the kitchen, he said, "Hey, Lori, why are you home—"

Then he froze in the doorway. A little girl with short dark braids was sitting at the table, eating a banana. She grinned, revealing two missing top teeth.

"Want a banana?" she said.

Chap stared.

"There's another one over there," she said, pointing vaguely behind her.

Chap continued to stare.

"I'm Peggy. I'm a surprise!" she announced.

Someone behind him laughed. Turning quickly, he faced an almost-Lori—a petite woman with short dark curly hair, a radiant smile, and dark playful eyes.

"Catherine?"

"That would be me, and you are my 'little' brother."

She laughed again. "Why on earth does my sister keep using that description for you?"

"Habit, I suppose. A bad habit."

"Well, little brother or not, I need a hug," she said.

Sliding off her chair, Peggy came around the table to join them. "Did we surprise you, Uncle Chap? Our job was to surprise you."

"That you did."

* * *

As Chap and Catherine worked to prepare a supper of barbecued chicken, baked potatoes, cooked cabbage, and a fruit salad, Peggy colored on the coffee table in the living room in the Disney book Lori had bought for her.

Chap was almost immediately comfortable both working and talking with Catherine—which surprised him since she was basically a stranger, but she was a stranger who resembled Lori. It was not only how Catherine looked but also how she laughed. Then, when she asked him to cut up the cabbage and he said, "Good Lord, do I now have another big sister to boss me around!" she wrinkled up her nose at him as Lori so often did.

She didn't seem to mind when Chap asked, "What have you been doing for the past ten years?"

He listened while she answered, feeling as he had when he and Lori had talked and cooked together in the kitchen in the big old house in Indiana.

"I knew I'd made a mistake with John within a year or so after we left Riverwoods. He wanted a carefree life, moving here and there, going from one job to another. If the people around us or the job or the place got boring—and he seemed to get bored very easily—we simply packed the car with our few possessions and hit the road."

"Why didn't you come home?"

"Pride—stupid pride."

"But our father would've let you come back, right?"

"Yes, I'm sure he would've. Even when I was maddest at him for being so strict, I never doubted that he loved us all. I never asked him because I didn't want to admit I'd made a mistake."

Catherine continued her story. John had been very unhappy when she'd gotten pregnant, and one night about two months before Peggy was born, he left.

"Peggy has never seen her father, but every once in a while a cashier's check comes. I bank it to give us a little cushion."

"So you're divorced, but you don't have regular support or a visitation agreement?" Chap asked.

Suddenly, Catherine quit talking. She frowned. Chap waited, wondering what he'd said that was wrong.

Finally, she said softly, "I'm not divorced because I never got married."

"You eloped."

"No, we didn't. We just claimed we did because the lie was easier than the truth."

Chap put the cabbage into a skillet with some olive oil and a bit of water. Neither he nor Catherine spoke for a while.

"Uncle Chap," Peggy called from the living room, "can you come color with me?"

"Go ahead," said Catherine. "We're all done here for now. We'll set the table later."

Sitting down on the floor beside Peggy, Chap started to color Mickey Mouse, who was dressed in a kilt and playing bagpipes.

Catherine perched on the arm of the couch and watched. Then turning to Peggy, she said, "Tell Uncle Chap your real name and how old you are."

"I'm Peggy Adele Smith, almost like Mommy—she's Catherine Adele Smith, and I'm six and a half," she said, emphasizing *half*.

"Well, I'm Charles Henry Anthony Peter Smith, and I'll be seventeen in about two months."

"So you're older. I don't care. I like being six and a half," Peggy declared, wrinkling up her nose.

Good Lord, Chap thought as he smiled, do all Smith females wrinkle up their noses?

Fifteen minutes later, Chap laid down his navy crayon and studied the plaid kilt he'd just finished.

"What do you think, Peggy? Does Mickey look good?"

"He does, Uncle Chap. You're a good colorer."

"Thank you, Ma'am, for the compliment."

Peggy giggled. "I'm not a man. I'm a girl.

Catherine grinned. "Let's go finish dinner. Lori and Doug will be here soon."

Back in the kitchen, out of Peggy's earshot, Catherine quietly picked up her story.

"When I wrote home, I never said that John was gone, but Dad guessed the truth. Then one day he called. We talked for a long time as he helped me figure out what I should do with a baby and a low-paying waitress job which barely kept a roof over our heads. In the end, he sent me a whopping big check, and I got a bachelor's degree in elementary education. Now I'm teaching second grade."

"You sure made that sound easy!" Chap said as he took the glass lid off the cabbage and flipped it over with a spatula.

Catherine snorted. "Hardly! Couldn't have done it at all without Nana Lee, my neighbor, whose own kids and grandkids are scattered all over the country. She fell in love with Peggy as soon as I brought her home from the hospital. She was going to watch her for nothing, but I insisted on paying her some. Then I started buying groceries for her because she kept feeding me. I'd come to get Peggy after class or my shift at the café, and she'd say, 'Why don't you have a bite to eat? I have a meatloaf in the oven.'"

Catherine smiled. "She was my angel."

"Did you go to college full-time?"

"Not quite. I knew I'd have to work some. The question was how much. I spent a weekend with a legal pad and a pencil, adding up the rent for my dinky, one-bedroom apartment, the utilities, groceries, diapers, gas, and insurance. At least my nine-year-old Honda was paid for. I also became a regular at the Goodwill store in the neighborhood. Then I added in tuition and guessed what books would cost. From that total, I subtracted what Dad had sent which gave me the shortfall. I ended up working about fifteen hours a week at the café."

Chap grinned. "I'm impressed—just with your math, which isn't my strong suit. Did it work as you'd planned?"

"It did. I skimped on sleep and anything not an absolute necessity and loaded up on coffee. I took a little less than a full load each semester, but I went year round—even taking intersession classes on-line. I graduated in four years."

Chap gave her a high five.

"Can I ask you something—something I've been wondering about recently?" he said.

"Of course, but I may not know the answer."

"Where did our father get enough money to raise us all? We weren't rich or anything, but there was always enough for what we needed. Plus you and Julianna have bachelor's degrees, and Lori finished an associate's degree. He always talked about me going to college as if I automatically would. How did he do all that on his retirement from the military?"

"Ah, so you never knew," Catherine said. "I didn't either until he started pushing me to take college prep classes when I was in high school.

Once night when we were arguing about who only knows what, I yelled, 'We can't even afford to have decent TV reception. How on earth are you going to pay for college?'

"Well, he very quietly ordered us four girls to sit down at the kitchen table—you were probably already in bed. Then he told us about our mother's inheritance. She was an only child, and when her mother died, she got a substantial amount of money, which she and Dad invested for our education. Besides that, before he and Mom were married, he'd inherited the falling-down house in Michigan and the surrounding four acres of woods, which at the time had seemed worthless. He had the house torn down, but he kept the acres. I don't know why since he never seemed sentimental about anything related to his growing up years. Anyway, about twenty years later, urban sprawl made those acres prime land for part of a new subdivision, and he got a lot of money for them.

"He made it very clear that night that he expected all of us to go to college like he and Mom hadn't done."

"Is much of that money left, besides what Lori got for the house?" Chap asked.

"Enough for all five of us to have a cushion. His will was written after Julianna, Marilee, and I had left home. Since you were still so young and Lori was at home, he stipulated that you two should have a larger share—Lori for running the house and you for college. Julianna, Marilee, and I will divide the rest."

"That's okay with you—not to have an even five-way split?"

"Oh, sure. I've felt plenty guilty for leaving home, especially when I knew later that Lori was taking care of so much. Julianna feels the same way even though she didn't run away like I did. Besides, we both have already gotten help with college expenses. Who knows what Marilee thinks since no one knows where she is."

Catherine explained that she was going to use her share to start a college fund for Peggy and a retirement fund for herself. The will even stipulated that Marilee's share would be kept for five years from the date of their father's death and then divided among the four siblings if she was not found.

"You know," Catherine said, "I wonder if Dad sensed that he'd die young. Sixty-two is very young for a man in good physical shape like he was. It's almost like he knew that you would still need money to go to college and that Marilee's whereabouts would be unknown."

No one spoke for a while.

Then Catherine said, "Why haven't you asked Lori about all of this?"

"I don't know exactly. I knew Lori had been handling our father's money for years before he died. It just seemed natural for her to handle the will and everything afterwards, too."

"That makes sense."

Peggy stomped into the kitchen and announced, "I'm hungry. I've washed my hands, and I'm ready to set the table."

With a flip of her braids, she turned toward the cupboard where her mother handed her five dinner plates.

"Napkins on the left, Peggy, under the forks," Chap said.

With great indignity, she replied, "I know. I've been setting the table since I was four and making my own bed since I was five and folding my own clothes since I was six."

Chap grinned. He was going to like this little kid.

***

The next morning, Peggy and Catherine boarded the city bus with Chap. Twenty minutes later, when they transferred to the second bus,

Chap introduced them to Miss Dorothea, who immediately got their life story during the remainder of the bus ride.

During supper the night before, Catherine had been fascinated with Chap's description of the Academy.

"I've got to see this place," she'd said. "But I need to be home by three to meet Julianna when she arrives from the airport."

"That's fine. We can leave whenever you want to."

"You can leave, too?" she said, eyebrows raised.

Chap explained the "loose" schedule he followed.

"Like I said, I *have* to see this place!"

Once they'd checked in with Miss Celia and gotten visitor badges, they went to the Language Arts Center for homeroom. After Chap introduced them, Branson offered to give Catherine a tour while Peggy joined a reading group.

When Catherine returned, she began to observe all the activities as kids came and went all morning. She sat in with a YAK Phonics group and helped an older group of six with vocabulary development using common roots, suffixes, and prefixes. She discussed the project that Chap, Keya, and Shannon were currently working on. She looked at some of the students' writing portfolios and reading records.

By the time she, Peggy, Chap, Owen, and De met for lunch, she was almost speechless. "I wouldn't have believed this if I hadn't seen it myself," she said, smiling and shaking her head.

She sounded like Chap had felt in June.

* * *

That evening Chap listened to his three sisters talking and laughing non-stop—the one he'd always known and the two who were new. After twenty-four hours with Catherine and Peggy, he felt he was truly related to them, and it didn't take him long to appreciate Julianna's quieter personality. She seemed to be more like he was—less verbal than her sisters but no less fun-loving.

There were lots of stories that started with "Remember when?" and more than one of them involved Chap. At age three, he'd drunk shampoo one morning. Hours later at suppertime, his father lectured him about not drinking things like that because they'd make him sick. Chap frowned and said, "When?" He'd drunk shampoo hours earlier, and he wasn't sick yet. Their father had smiled when he said, "This one is going to be another smart Smith."

Then there was the time they'd driven to town when it was so hot that they could hear their tires sticking to First Woods Road. His father said that the asphalt was actually melting in the heat. When Chap asked, "What's asphalt?" Marilee quipped, "It's the crack in your butt." That remark had caused great hilarity in the car and then a twenty-four-hour grounding to her room for Marilee.

"And then there was the time, around Thanksgiving, I think," Julianna said, "when you said at the supper table, 'Soon I can hold up my thumb.' You seemed to be so pleased with yourself, but we didn't have a clue about what you meant. When we asked, you just repeated, 'Soon I can hold up my thumb.' Finally, I asked you to show us what you meant. You stuck out your hand with four fingers up and your thumb folded back. Then you spread all five fingers wide. Your fifth birthday was coming up in January."

By the time everyone headed to bed, Chap felt that he truly had a much bigger family—not just one sister but three and a cute little niece who was already sound asleep on the pull-out couch. Tomorrow he'd add a brother. Just a year ago, he'd written about all who'd left him in the paper for Mrs. Hunt—his mother, his older sisters, even the heron at the wooden bridge over Wandering River. Now his mother and father were gone, but through the eyes of his sisters, he was getting to know them both much better. Some pieces of his life were gone forever, but others he was finding.

* * *

November 18

Dear Erica,

Home alone! Didn't they make a movie or two or three with that title?

Doug and Lori are due back Saturday afternoon from their honeymoon in the mountains in Tennessee where it's peaceful with the summer tourists and most of the fall leaf-viewers gone. They call every day to see if I'm still alive! Like I didn't take care of myself last year when I was fifteen and Lori was gone for months.

Anyway, the wedding was perfect. Lori invited Owen, who came with De, of course, and Miss April. The boys looked so serious, sitting in the second row in their white shirts and ties, definitely on their best behavior. Those two little guys are really special.

Julianna and Catherine wore matching long-sleeved burnt orange dresses and carried bouquets of yellow flowers and fall leaves. Lori was beautiful in her elegant gown. Doug, his best friend, and I wore black suits—no tuxedos or frilly shirts or colorful cummerbunds, thank goodness. A friend of Lori's from work sang several solos, and the minister gave a short message about the importance of learning to grow and change together over the coming years.

I've often wondered about that. People change, so how do couples manage to stay together when the two people who marry won't be the same people ten or twenty or fifty years down the road?

The minister's answer was that in dedicated couples, each one weighs changes in light of the other and neither makes decisions that will cause pain or separation. That's a pretty simple summary, but do you get what he was saying?

He also talked about doors in life. When we make decisions, we often open one door but close others. He gave Doug an example. He said, "You've opened the door to living with a wonderful beautiful woman, but, if you're smart, you've closed the door to staring at certain other women's anatomical parts, especially when you and Lori are together." We all laughed out loud at that, and I swear that Doug turned red.

Anyway, I missed sharing the lovely day with you. As Lori walked down the aisle on Doug's father's arm, I wondered if someday I might be standing in Doug's spot, watching you walk toward me.

I know, I know. We're too young to know what we'll want or who we'll love when we're older, but I still pictured you walking down the aisle. . . .

Love you, Chap

P.S. You know that part of the ceremony when the minister asks, "Who shall give away this woman?"—or something like that—and the bride's father says, "Her mother and I."

Well, this time the minister asked, "Who has escorted this young woman to the altar?" and Doug's father replied, "I have so that she can become a wonderful new member of our family." I thought that was neat!

Chapter 12

It's not that it never snows in Virginia. It's just that it snows so infrequently that drivers seem to forget between times how to drive when it's slick. So that morning in early January, Miss Dorothea was uncharacteristically quiet as she slowly maneuvered the bus through the crowded streets.

The two-week winter break was over, and Chap was eager to get back to school. He remembered wanting to return to Riverwoods High after Lori had moved to Virginia and he was alone with his father, but there was a difference then. His desire to be at school was more to escape from the silence and loneliness with his reticent father at home.

Now he simply wanted to go to school. There was nothing unpleasant at home. Rather quickly, Lori, Doug, and Chap had established a family routine that worked for the three of them. Chap, who usually got home first, did his chores—they'd divided up the weekly laundry-cleaning tasks—and then he'd start some part of supper like peeling potatoes or making salad or putting something in the oven. When Lori and Doug got home, all three of them would finish the meal prep. After supper, they did something together for an hour or so as they'd done in the little apartment. Then Chap would go to his room to read or write letters or study.

"Hey, buddy, it's slick out there," Miss Dorothea yelled at a driver who'd pulled out of a side street in front of her. Oblivious, the man drove on, fishtailing just a bit as he sped ahead.

At Chap's stop, she said, with a frown, "Be careful out there. It's icy. Tell Owen 'hi' for me. I sure miss that little kid."

As Chap walked to the Academy, he looked at the snow—so different in a city than in the Indiana woods. There is stayed on the ground unblemished, sometimes for days, but here it was immediately tarnished by the dirty slush thrown up by vehicle tires and snowplows. People shoveled walks, and dogs pranced outside in yards to do their thing. Within hours of a snowfall, the pristine look was gone.

Once inside the Academy, Chap typed his name to sign in for the day. Both De and Owen beamed when he walked into the Language Arts Center. Homeroom was a bit longer than usual as several told about holiday travels. Then he slid right back into the routine he'd established. He was reading *Roots* by Alex Haley for the next part of his American history-literature work. He'd started a new science unit that dealt with how various species had successfully or unsuccessfully adapted to environmental changes. The algebra review was going well; he planned to start geometry after spring break with a group of six other seniors. He also had Spanish, another semester of music on-line, and basketball again. Added to that was his time helping with the laundry and tutoring in the Language Arts Center.

More and more, Chap wondered if he'd found his career—becoming a teacher, maybe even helping to start another Academy somewhere, some day. Miss Sydney frequently introduced adults in homeroom who were there to observe. More than once, Chap had been asked to let a visitor shadow him for a day or two. There were people out there interested in what was happening inside the Academy.

* * *

January 19

Dear Tom,

Remember how I used to brag about being the oldest kid in our class. Well, once again, I'm seventeen before any of the rest of you. So there!

What a difference a year makes! Remember what happened on my sixteenth birthday? The day was normal, but that night was when I found my father in the snow after he'd wandered away. He was never in our house again. Lori came home, and he went from the hospital to a nursing home and finally to the VA Hospital. Then after school was out, we moved to Virginia and I started going to the Academy.

Some parts of last year seem like yesterday, but a lot of it seems like years ago. It's hard to believe that on my sixteenth birthday I didn't know Owen or De or even Doug. Almost all the pieces of my life are new now.

You asked in your last email if Lori has changed her name. The answer is yes. With a huge grin, she said to Doug, "You're smart enough to know you won't own me, but I do like your last name." I guess years ago when a woman got married, she kind of became her husband's property along with anything she actually did own. Lori said that is why some women now keep their own name after they marry—a feminist thing. Anyway, she is now Loretta Elizabeth Smith Van Wyck. That's Dutch, I think. Aren't lots of Dutch people blue-eyed and blonde like Doug? I'll have to ask him.

Have you thought at all about what you'll do after high school? If I can get all the math done, I should meet high school graduation requirements here about the same time you do—a year from June. I'm thinking about college in Illinois. Don't say it. I already know it's because of Erica. I sure hope she doesn't choose to go to someplace even farther away like Maine or Montana or New Mexico!

Tell the guys at the lunch table hello. I do like this school, but I miss all of you.

Your buddy, Chap

* * *

Winter continued on with just a few more dirty, depressing snows. At the Academy, De's "library" of books he could read by himself now numbered twenty-three. He kept the list, laboriously copying each title onto a sheet of paper, in his progress folder. Owen was walking most of the day, using a wheelchair that was kept at the Academy only when his legs got too tired in the afternoon. Because he diligently took home extra math problems every night, he'd mastered basic computation skills for addition, subtraction, multiplication, and division. He was constantly asking people to give him a problem. One day when Chap said, "30,321 divided by 9," Owen said, "That's too easy. I'll divide it by 19."

Someone discovered that De had perfect pitch and loved to sing. De later admitted that his grandpa had sung with a band in his youth. That was the first positive thing he'd ever said about his family. Owen liked to draw. Soon both had added those activities to their basic curriculum of reading, writing, and math. Owen was also doing independent science and social studies projects since he could read so well. Independent study would come later for De.

The real change for the boys was the addition of a foster baby to the family—a cute round-faced four-month-old baby girl. She'd been abandoned at a fire station without even a name. The O'Neills had decided to call her Rose because of her chubby, rosy cheeks and reddish-brown hair. At first, both boys had grumbled about all the attention she got, but within a few weeks, they were dropping by the nursery to see her before they went to lunch.

At that time, Chap decided he should meet the Academy's requirement of a semester-long child development class which included spending a minimum of two hours a week with the babes and little ones.

He decided not to tell Tom about that new addition to his schedule, but he did tell Erica on the phone one night.

"How do you know what to do when you get there?" she asked.

"There's a white board that lists what needs to be done. I choose one from the top three since they're listed by need."

"So what did you do yesterday?"

"I rocked baby Rose to sleep after I gave her a bottle. She's teething and miserable a lot right now. Miss April is threatening to kidnap me since Rose falls asleep easily when I rock her."

"I don't know," Erica said. "I'm having trouble picturing you rocking a baby. Actually, I'm having trouble picturing any teenagers I know working with babies and little kids."

"I know. That's why I'm certainly not going to tell Tom!"

Erica laughed. "Okay, so tell me what you did the time before that?"

"I read to Alex and Toby. They're three. Then I sat on the floor and helped them build a tower with colored blocks. I let them tell me what to do which encourages them to verbalize. I ask them what color should I use and which kinds of blocks. If they only point, I'm supposed to say, 'Tell me what color,' or 'Tell me what size.' That way they learn the primary colors very early and some basic shapes, too."

"There's a child development class here, an elective," Erica said, "but I don't know anyone who's taking it. I like the idea that everyone there has to work with kids. Most of us will be parents someday yet almost none of us will have had classes related to parenting or hands-on practice like you're getting."

Chap was quiet for a bit, and then he said, "Do you want to have children someday?"

Erica laughed. "Why did I know you'd ask? Do you think about anything else besides getting married and having kids?"

Chap didn't respond, and the silence got long.

Then Erica said softly, "I'm sorry, Chap. I don't mean to make fun of you. It's just that making adult decisions like marriage and kids seems too far away for me to think about much." She paused and then added, "But when I do, I have trouble thinking about anyone else except you."

"Good night, Erica."

Chap's heart was pounding when he turned off the phone.

***

Journal Entry #9 - March 23

Do you remember when I wrote my autobiography entitled "Loss"? I think I was feeling particularly deserted because Lori had gone to Virginia. What a difference in my family now. I told you before about Catherine and Peggy coming from California and Julianna from Missouri for Lori's wedding. Well, we've become a lot closer since then. Peggy writes me funny little notes in the letters Catherine sends every month. When Catherine calls, she talks to both Lori and me on the speaker. Last weekend, Julianna decided to bring her boyfriend to meet us. Judging from the way they are together, I'm guessing there will be another wedding soon. Greg is also artistic, a graphic designer.

Spring is finally starting to arrive. Since we have no idea what is planted around our house and in the backyard, we are looking every day for signs. Lori recognized the flat leaves of daffodils around the front stoop, and some shrubs along the back fence look like they may be forsythia. So far the grass in the yard is mostly brownish, which is good since mowing has been designated as my chore. Doug will trim and edge, and Lori snatched the flower job—the easiest one.

Now here's the really big news. Our two-week break is coming up soon, and I'm flying to San Diego to spend three days with Peggy and Catherine during their spring break. My first time west of the Mississippi, my first time traveling alone, my first time flying. I'm a nervous wreck!

Hope your school year is going well. Mine is. I think I'll be in line to graduate on time since the math is progressing. I'm cramming remedial work, algebra review, geometry, and advanced algebra into two years here. That would be impossible without tutoring and being able to move at my own pace, which, believe it or not, has picked up a lot. It's funny how when the fear of not doing well disappeared, I quit disliking math. I still don't love it like I do reading and writing, but I don't dread time in the Math Center.

I'm thinking about becoming a teacher. What do you think?

Chapter 13

Chap wiped his hands on his jeans for the tenth time. Minutes ago, the pilot had told them all to remain seated and fasten their seat belts. They would be landing at O'Hare in about thirty minutes. As he stared out the little window, the plane dropped gradually from above the sea of fluffy sunlit white clouds into a disappointing dismal gray fog. Every time the plane bucked or shuddered, he grasped the armrests until his knuckles were white. Even so, he was trying to appear nonchalant since he was sitting next to a pretty, red-haired college coed wearing a Northwestern sweatshirt. There were no white knuckles for her as she read and highlighted passages in a large psychology text open on her lap.

Suddenly, the plane was beneath the clouds with Chicago spread out below. Chap could see Lake Michigan in the far distance and what appeared to be a sports stadium. Tiny, ant-sized cars streamed on roads crisscrossing everywhere. Neighborhoods looked tidy with roofs all lined up. He wondered if he was seeing where Erica lived. As the plane dropped lower, he could detect the hint of spring green in the new leaves. Finally, the cars got bigger and bigger, and he could distinguish red ones from black ones from white ones. Many huge warehouse roofs and a gigantic railroad yard appeared as the plane got closer to the airport.

When the plane bumped down, Chap's stomach lurched. Then the brownish grass along the runway flew by even as the pilot jammed on the brakes. Chap squinched his eyes closed until the plane had slowed to taxiing speed. Minutes later, it crossed other runways and approached a terminal where all kinds of planes were lined up.

When the plane stopped, passengers began to jam the narrow aisle. With cell phones in hand, they were announcing their safe landing and arranging meeting places. Since he was too tall to stand beneath the overhead bin, Chap sat.

The girl next to him spoke for the first time. "Are you staying in Chicago?"

"No, I'm going to visit my sister in San Diego."

"That's nice," she replied. "Have a good time."

She stood and turned her back to him. Chap figured that she'd completed all that she considered necessary for a conversation with a seatmate she'd never see again, but it felt odd to him to have sat so close to someone for a couple of hours and not to know even her name.

When the front doors of the plane opened, the queue of baggage-laden passengers slowly began to move down the aisle. The girl left first. Then Chap politely let several from behind go past before he stepped into the aisle. At the front of the plane, he was bid farewell by one pilot and other crew members. Then he proceeded down what looked like a tunnel to the waiting areas, where hundreds of people were milling around—many walking by quickly, many more standing to board other planes.

After checking a huge electronic board, he found his next flight number with "On time" beside it. Even so, he had a two-hour wait in front of him. He mentally reviewed Lori's advice: "First, find your next gate. Then locate a nearby restroom. Finally, get something to eat since airplane food for passengers flying cheap consists of a snack, maybe, and a drink or two."

With that in mind, he headed down the center of the terminal, looking at the overhead signs to guide him to his next gate. He cataloged the location of a McDonald's and a deli as his stomach growled. After a long hike, he found his new gate, checked again to see about his time of departure on another board. Noting the row of clocks above the board which listed times in various places around the world, he flipped open the inexpensive phone Lori had purchased for the trip to make sure that the time there matched the time on the clock marked Chicago. Then he headed back to the deli for a sandwich.

Later, with his stomach satisfied, he sat in the waiting area, looking at the sea of humanity all around him—all ages, all colors, all manner of dress. The snippets of unfamiliar languages he heard made him wonder just how many nationalities passed through O'Hare on a typical day in March. Turning around, he looked out the floor-to-ceiling windows at Chicago, but all he could see were runways and lots of planes taxiing to and from various gates. Somewhere, beyond all that, was Erica. This was her city.

* * *

Shortly after the plane reached cruising altitude—Chap didn't even want to think about how high up they were—the skies cleared, and Chap could see the farmland below. Before his seatmate, a round-faced Catholic priest with light-blue eyes and a friendly smile, had fallen asleep, he'd explained that the deep green fields had been planted the previous fall with winter wheat and the dark ones were still unplanted.

Even though Chap's father had insisted Chap learn all fifty states and their capitals when he was ten, Chap couldn't determine exactly where he was. The Mississippi River had been clearly visible not long after the plane left Chicago, but after that, he was unsure about which states he was seeing from above—probably Kansas with lots of green fields, maybe Colorado and Utah where the mountains were spectacular with jagged snow-covered peaks.

At one point, the pilot interrupted everyone's naps, reading, or television viewing to announce over the crackly radio that they were flying over the Grand Canyon, which looked colorful but not so amazing with the depth perception lost from miles above. That information meant the plane was flying over Arizona for sure and probably the southern tip of Nevada, too. His seatmate, who'd awakened during the announcement about the Grand Canyon, explained why Chap was seeing some round fields below.

"Those are irrigated fields with wells in the center and long arms that move slowly in circles to sprinkle crops from above," he said.

Later Chap felt the plane beginning to descend. As they neared the coast, the mountains were more barren looking with little snow on them. Finally, San Diego came into view. The descent into the city was lovely with so much green below and the early afternoon sun glinting off the Pacific Ocean.

After deplaning, Chap followed the crowd to the unmoving baggage carousel. As he stood there, his thumping heart began to slow. His brain was on overload, but he felt exhausted. The clocks at the airport indicated that it was mid-afternoon, but Chap's body said it was supper time. Through the magic of flight, he was going to have a twenty-seven hour day.

With a jerk and a loud rumble, the carousel began to move, disgorging all manner of luggage from a large square opening covered with strips of what appeared to be black rubber. Lori had tied a piece of heavy blue yarn to her otherwise generic-looking black suitcase. He was glad since it seemed that every other bag was black. The belt carrying the luggage looped around and then disappeared back through a low entrance, taking with it the bags not claimed on its first circuit. New ones continued to tumble from the opening. Chap carefully squeezed his way up closer to the moving belt, finally spying his bag with the blue yarn coming around the bend. After grabbing it, he double checked the tag number.

Then he headed outside to meet Catherine. He saw her before she saw him. Actually, he heard Peggy first.

"But why are we here, Mommy? Are we going on a trip again?"

When they got closer, Chap stepped in front of them and said, with a huge grin, "Surprise!"

Peggy squealed and flew into his arms.

* * *

Chap stared and stared as San Diego flashed by the car windows. The freeway was six lanes wide in places and curved all around. The residential streets were lined with huge shaggy-barked eucalyptus trees and tall palms. Most of the small houses were buried in colorful shrubs and flowers.

"What's that purple flower that climbs up lots of the houses?" he asked.

"That's buggy vine," said Peggy. "Isn't it pretty? We have some at our house."

"Actually, it's bougainvillea," Catherine said with a laugh. "Are you hungry?"

"Sure am. I ate only a chicken sandwich at O'Hare because I didn't want to be too full. My stomach isn't such a good flyer, so far."

"Let's stop for some food before we go to the house. How's Chinese food?"

"I've never eaten much of that type of food, but it sounds good."

"That's 'cause it is good," said Peggy with a grin that showed the two new teeth that had been growing in since the wedding.

Minutes later, they left a small restaurant in a strip mall with several boxes of steaming food, and minutes after that, they were sitting at a shaded picnic table, which was perched on a small bluff that overlooked the ocean. Catherine spread out a green and white checked tablecloth and retrieved a thermos of mixed fruit juices from the trunk of the car.

Below, on the beach, a group of kids ran up and down, flying big brightly colored kites of all sorts. Two figures in shiny black suits bobbed on the ocean as they waited for a wave to ride into the shore. Lots of other people walked along the beach—some with leashed dogs, some in pairs, some alone.

Long after the food was gone, Chap and Catherine sat and talked while Peggy dug holes in the sand just below them.

"How did you end up in San Diego after so many years in Portland?" Chap asked.

"I was afraid you'd ask that at some point," Catherine said with a frown.

"That's okay. I don't need to know."

"Oh, you might as well. I wouldn't want you to think I'm the perfect older sister," she said with a wry smile. "A man. I left home with a man— big mistake except that I have Peggy, who is the joy of my life. I came to San Diego because of a man—second big mistake.

"I met Bryan at a tenth-anniversary party. He'd gone to college with the host, and I taught in the same school with the hostess. Bryan was from San Diego, but he traveled all up and down the coast for his job. He's a rep for a company that makes prostheses."

When Catherine paused, Chap said, "So far, I don't see the big mistake."

"Like, duh—neither did I for over a year! We saw each other regularly whenever he was in Portland. Peggy adored him, and he seemed to adore her. We talked about our goals, our political and religious views. There were no red flags. My whole life began to revolve around the time we were together—a few days about once a month. He kept saying that he wished we lived closer to each other.

"Then on Valentine's Day a year ago he proposed, and I said yes. But he didn't want to set a wedding date. That should've been my first clue. The second should've been that I had no address or home phone number for him. 'No need,' he'd say, 'since I'm rarely there. You have my cell.'"

Catherine shook her head. "In my case, love didn't make me just blind but also dumb as a post."

She paused and looked down at Peggy, who was digging a hole big enough to sit in. Chap didn't know what to say, so he said nothing.

"What's really pathetic is that I truly thought I was planning well, not just being impulsive like I'd been when I'd left home with John. I figured that when we got married, I'd have to move, so why not do it before then so that we could be together more often. That was my reasoning.

"Without telling Bryan or anyone else, I made a quick trip to San Diego in late April. I left Peggy with Nana Lee. I actually found the house to share immediately, and after I paid a deposit, my roommates were willing to keep the room until June. I got leads on three teaching jobs for fall. I even rented a small storage unit.

"Two days after the end of the school year, I resigned. That way no one would know I was leaving. We packed our meager belongings and odds and ends of furniture into a U-Haul and said good-bye to Nana Lee, which was the hardest part. I'm not sure I could've done it except that she was moving, too, to Louisville to be nearer her youngest daughter.

"Anyway, I'd gotten Bryan's address from my friend's husband in Portland, so a couple of days after we'd gotten settled into the house, I left Peggy with the roommates one evening and drove to Bryan's house to surprise him. Well, imagine my surprise when *his wife* answered the doorbell with two little kids hanging onto her legs. The son of a bitch is married!"

Catherine's hand flew to her mouth.

"Sorry about that. I try to keep my language under control, but thoughts of him seem to remove my censors."

"What did you say to his wife?"

"I have no clue how I kept my composure, but I pretended to be a co-worker. I don't remember exactly what I said, but I do remember hiding my left hand with the engagement ring behind my back."

"Why didn't you tell her who you really were?"

"I don't know," Catherine said with a shrug. "She just seemed to be so nice. . . ."

Chap smiled at his sister.

"Before you pin a halo on me, I have to admit that I left my real name and cell number with her."

Chap's smile got wider.

"Then I went back to the car, drove two blocks, pulled over, and cried for an hour."

Chap's smile faded. The pain in Catherine's voice was cutting.

"Did he call you?"

"Oh, yeah. That he did. He started to say, 'Let me explain—' but I cut him off. I said, 'You're married, you son of a bitch.' Then I hung up. I was too embarrassed to tell him I was in San Diego."

Chap and Catherine silently stared at the ocean. The sun was getting low in the Western sky, turning the high fleecy clouds peach colored and the wave crests gold.

"Do you plan to stay in San Diego?"

"Probably not. I love the climate, and I like my teaching job, but there's no sense of community here. People are always moving—if not from city to city, at least from one house or apartment to another. Most everybody works and the commute times are often long, so people aren't home much except on weekends, and then most are busy with activities and chores."

"I know what you mean," Chap said. "In the city, I'm surrounded by people, but I feel lonelier there than I did when I was actually alone in the woods in Indiana. In the city, it seems like people don't want to invest the time and attention friendship takes when they know that any connection is likely to be temporary. Why get to know your neighbor when either one of you is likely to move soon? And the likelihood of keeping in touch is remote because you had no real connection to start with."

"Wow, Chap, you've sure nailed the problem, and you've lived in a city for less than a year! I'm impressed."

Looking down at the little figure below them, Catherine called, "Two more minutes, Peggy."

"Aw, Mommy."

"Don't 'Aw, Mommy' me. You know the rule."

Peggy stood up, put her hands on her hips, and stared at the ocean as if trying to decide whether or not to protest further. Apparently, she did know the rule, and the consequences weren't worth the risk. With a frown, she dumped the sand from her little blue pail with the yellow octopus on the side and brushed off the sand.

As Peggy slowly trudged up the weathered wooden steps, Catherine smiled as she whispered, "She knows that getting to come back soon depends on her cooperating, but I'm not too picky about how cheerfully she does so."

Catherine gathered the trash and folded up the tablecloth. She took a towel from the trunk and wiped the sand off Peggy's legs and feet. The pail, rake, and shovel went into a plastic tub. It was apparent that they were prepared for beach time just about any time.

Ten minutes later, they pulled into the driveway of a small pale-green house with a huge "buggy vine" growing near the front door. Chap stepped into the open living room-kitchen area where two ladies, whom Catherine had called her "great roommates," were eating supper. Catherine introduced them. MayCee was a tall, slender black lady with a bushy pony tail who looked enough like Miss Sydney to be her sister, and Lily was a fortyish lady with spiky gray hair.

After a few minutes of getting-acquainted chit-chat, Catherine said to Chap, "Let's get you settled in. Your eyes say it's way past eight o'clock for you."

Chap would sleep on the pull-out sofa and share a bathroom with Catherine and Peggy, who had the largest of the three bedrooms.

"See my bed, Uncle Chap," Peggy said as she pulled a little trundle from under her mother's single bed. Then pointing first to a large table, covered with books and papers, and then to a much smaller one, she added, "And I have my own study table, just like Mommy's."

"It's overly cozy, if you know what I mean, but it'll do for now," Catherine said. "Another reason I won't stay here is real estate values. On a teacher's salary, I could never qualify to buy a house, even one as tiny as this."

"Really!" Chap exclaimed.

"Yes, really. I'd have to go inland a long ways to buy anything, and then I'd be facing a long commute in bumper-to-bumper traffic. Besides, what's the use of living in an ocean-side city if you aren't close to the ocean? What I'd like to do is move to a place where Peggy and I can put down real roots with stable neighbors, a local church, and a grocery store where we'll run into people we know like we used to do in Riverwoods, some place where a drive to work isn't grueling."

"I think Lori and Doug are beginning to feel the same way," Chap said. "Doug has always lived near Washington, D.C., but he asks Lori a lot about our lives growing up in the woods and what a small city of thirty thousand is like."

Catherine laughed. "Maybe we should all move back to Indiana together."

Chap laughed, too, but his heart skipped a beat, just hearing the words.

Chapter 14

Peggy squealed. "We're almost there! We're almost there!"

Catherine grinned. "This is our one luxury. I bought annual passes. Peggy will be your guide since she knows the layout of the whole place."

The parking lot was huge with various animals on high signs marking the rows. Theirs was a giraffe. Decked out in a sundress of large red and white checks and red ribbons at the ends of her dark braids, Peggy was literally prancing around her mother, trying to get her to move toward the entrance just a little bit faster.

This was the famous San Diego Zoo, which Chap had seen only on television a time or two. Actually, he'd never been to any zoo, not the one in Indianapolis nor the National Zoo in Washington. Within minutes, he knew why Peggy loved it.

"There's a million animals here, Uncle Chap," she said as she waved at the flamingos wading in a pond just inside the entrance.

"Actually, it's more like 3700," Catherine said, "on about 100 acres."

Peggy grabbed Chap's hand and pulled him toward one of the monkey cages where little creatures scampered and swung all around inside. Wee babies clung to their mothers, their wide eyes staring at all the strange creatures on the outside.

The orangutan was great fun as he sat like a wise dark-orange Buddha, studying those who stared at him. The elephants were massive as were the rhinoceroses whose dusty skin looked like armor. The giraffes moved with studied grace across their large enclosure, their six-foot babies by their sides. Two sun bears fought viciously over an ice cream cone someone had thrown into their pen. They spent a long time at the Polar Bear Plunge, watching the bears swim and looking at other species found in the Arctic.

When they came to the house of snakes, Chap suggested they go inside—before he saw Catherine, standing behind Peggy, vigorously shake her head no.

"Oh, let's see the snakes, Mommy. We always run out of time when we are here alone. Now we can go."

"Why don't you go with Uncle Chap while I wait outside and enjoy the sunshine."

As Peggy started inside, Chap mouthed, "Fraidy cat" at his older sister. She wrinkled up her nose at him.

The trick most of the time was to find the snakes, which were well camouflaged in the glass-fronted enclosures. As Chap read the information cards, Peggy searched for the snakes, squealing with delight whenever she spotted one. She was fascinated with their forked tongues, trying to comprehend that a snake's tongue acted something like a nose in sensing what was around it—food or a possible mate or even an enemy.

At the last large enclosure, Peggy only stared and stared. The two boa constrictors inside were huge. Their pinkish tan bodies with dark crossbars were partially coiled around tree branches and partially lying on the floor of the enclosure.

After reading the card, Chap said, "Did you know that the females are larger than the males?"

"Good for them," Peggy said as she pumped her arm in the air to show her approval of lady boas.

"They come from Africa, Asia, and Australia. They are very big, heavy-bodied snakes. Some females get as long as thirteen feet—that's two times longer than I am tall—and they can weigh sixty pounds—that's more than you weigh. But they aren't as big as some other snakes like anacondas and pythons."

"Wow!" was Peggy's response.

When they found Catherine outside, Peggy said only, "Well, that was something!"

Catherine and Chap grinned.

After Chap ate a quick sandwich, he left Peggy and Catherine to eat more leisurely while he went to see the tropical bird aviary with two hundred mostly colorful birds, according to the zoo pamphlet. He wanted to see real birds, not just ones in books or on videos. The pamphlet was right. There were birds in the aviary of every color and shape, large and small.

On the way back to where he'd left Peggy and Catherine, he saw tiny hummingbirds with eggs the size of peas and the California condor with a wing span of eight feet. White swans glided gracefully on a small pond. There were ducks of all kinds and birds of prey, including a bald eagle which stared at him with its golden eyes. The diversity was what intrigued him. Why were flamingos pink, and why did boobies have shockingly blue feet? Why did robins migrate and cardinals did not? Chap knew what some of the questions were that he was going to pursue when he returned to the Academy.

Back at the eating area, Catherine was sitting on a bench in the shade, reading her Nook. Peggy was asleep, her head on her mother's lap.

"Let's let her sleep another fifteen minutes. Then she'll want to take you to her favorite exhibit."

"What are you reading?"

"A Twin Rivers mystery by a guy from the Midwest—Illinois, I think. This is the second one. The first one was *One Last Shot*. This one is *A Shot after Midnight*, and I just got the third one, *Shot to Hell*. The mysteries are good, but the best part is the characters in the town of Twin Rivers. Lots of bad things happen, of course, but the people can be so funny. Anyway, I carry my Nook everywhere, just in case I'm stuck in traffic or have to wait for anything. You know, our father did a really good job of making readers out of all of us."

"I'm guessing that you're doing the same with Peggy."

Apparently, hearing her name awakened Peggy. She popped up like a jack-in-the-box, slid off the bench, and grabbed Chap's hand.

"Now it's time to see my favorite animals!"

As they headed down the path, Catherine said to Chap, "Sure wish I could wake up that fast."

Chap smiled.

* * *

The parking lot was no longer full when Peggy finally agreed to call it a day even though the map showed that they hadn't seen quite all of the zoo. They'd spent almost half an hour looking at Peggy's favorite, the koalas, though they seemed to do little except slowly munch on eucalyptus leaves and stare sleepily at the people pointing at them. They also went through a building where baby animals were being cared for by keepers. Peggy especially liked the baby chimp in a Luv diaper, sucking milk from a baby bottle.

After leaving the zoo, they ate sub sandwiches at a little neighborhood deli and then headed home to showers and bed. Peggy was asleep just minutes after she was tucked in with her terry cloth doll, Pink Baby, who was now more washed-out gray than pink, and her raggedy baby quilt.

* * *

The next morning, Peggy and Chap pulled a little wagon down the street to an orange tree that hung over the sidewalk. After Peggy rang the doorbell and introduced her Uncle Chap to the elderly Asian lady inside, the three of them used a long-handled gizmo to pull oranges off the top branches of her tree. When Chap and Peggy had filled their wagon and Mrs. Ito had filled her pail, they said good-bye and headed back up the street.

Chap had never squeezed fresh oranges or tasted fresh juice. He had one more thing to tell De and Owen about.

Later they packed peanut butter and jelly sandwiches, chips, kiwis, and more oranges into a picnic basket and headed to Catherine's favorite beach in La Jolla, which Chap pronounced correctly due to his Spanish class—"la hoya." They parked on a narrow street that curved along the shore. The waves were higher that day, and the roar of the ocean louder. Catherine had checked on the time when the tide would be high and then going out. They climbed down to a rocky area which the waves partially covered with foaming water every minute or so.

After they took off their shoes and socks and put them next to the wooden steps, Peggy said, "Be careful, Uncle Chap. It's slippery."

At first, Chap only noticed that the ocean and the rocks were beautiful. It wasn't until he looked more closely that he realized what made the beach so special. Over the millennia, the pounding waves had carved small cracks and rounded indentations into the dark-gray rocks. Inside those little tide pools were all sorts of creatures that depended on the waves to bring them their livelihood.

The three of them knelt by those pools for a long time, watching the waving antennae of the colorful sea anemones and the little shelled creatures. Then, after eating their picnic lunch, they went to a small shop that sold all sorts jewelry made from shells. Chap chose a necklace of flat white shells pieces shaped like triangles for Lori. Then they paid to enter a sea cave. They walked down a long damp staircase as the ocean mist rose from below them. At the bottom, they stood on a wooden platform in a deep cave as the waves roared in and then ebbed back out only to be met by other huge waves. The chaotic crashing made conversation impossible. When Peggy shivered, Chap reached down and picked her up.

"I love you, Uncle Chap," she said in his ear.

* * *

After a breakfast of more fresh juice, yogurt, and English muffins, Catherine and Peggy planned their last day together, Saturday—first shopping at an open-air mall and then time at a bay with an area called Mother's Beach where Peggy liked to wade and play on the swings.

Chap feigned enthusiasm for the plan even though he'd never cared much for shopping malls with their long, wide, shiny-tiled aisles and predictable shops. When he'd first gone to a mall in Virginia with Lori, he'd been somewhat dismayed to see many of the same stores that were in the mall in Riverwoods—the Gap, Bath and Body Works, Barnes and Noble, and Foot Locker, for example. He'd figured that if his life had to change so dramatically, he should at least have some totally new experiences. Shopping, it turned out, wasn't one of them.

After a short trip on a freeway, Catherine pulled into an underground parking garage where different areas were marked with fruit and veggies. As soon as they stepped out of the elevator into Horton Plaza, Chap knew that this was going to be like no other shopping trip he'd ever had. To say that every color of the rainbow hit his eyes was an understatement. It was a myriad of vibrant shades of every color and all sorts of geometric designs. The aisles angled all around with balconies jutting out here and there. On a tall pedestal in one area stood a huge Jessop clock, built in 1907, according to the plaque. Above the five levels of shops and restaurants—120 of them, Catherine said—was the blue sky and wispy white clouds.

"Wow!" was all that Chap said as he turned slowly around, looking up at the levels.

"Let's get started," Peggy said, pulling on Chap's hand. "I have shopping to do."

Catherine and Chap grinned.

Due to her limited finances, Catherine had told Peggy in the car that she could look for one thing that cost five dollars or less. As they meandered around the lowest level, Peggy began compiling a mental list of possibilities. Chap was doing the same, trying to decide what to buy for Catherine, Peggy, and himself. Some stores had familiar names like Victoria's Secret and Banana Republic, but many were little specialty shops for things like perfume and jewelry.

They continued to explore the second level and then the third. There Peggy found Crown Books and the section of chapter books. Chap went over to look at a nearby shop called Lids, which turned out to have all types of hats and other wearing apparel for the NFL, NHL, NBA, and MLB.

Various smells from the many restaurants had tempted them all morning, especially the aroma of freshly baked cinnamon buns. Finally, around one, they found Fish N Chips. They ate their lunches at an outside table on level three, close to a railing which allowed them to look down on the color and people below. After they finished lunch, Chap announced that he was going to buy sandals for all three of them from the sandal shop they'd seen on the second level.

Catherine asked Peggy, "Have you decided what you want to buy?"

Among the items Peggy had looked at closely as they'd browsed were bright pink flip-flops, bookmarks with animals on them, a flowered headband, and a chapter book.

"I'll show you," she said secretly as they dumped their trash into a nearby garbage can.

Following her lead, they returned to Crown Books where she headed for the Junie B. Jones books. After reading lots of titles aloud, she pulled *Junie B. Jones and the Stupid Smelly Bus* from the shelf. At the checkout counter, she proudly plopped down the book and her five-dollar bill. When the clerk told her the total was over five dollars, Peggy's eyes widened.

"It says $4.95 on the back," she said with a slight quaver in her voice.

Looking up, the clerk saw the hint of tears in her eyes and said gently, "You're right, but I have to add the tax."

"What's tax?"

"Never mind now, Peggy, I'll pay the tax. I can explain later," Catherine said.

Once her book was in a little white bag with handles, Peggy's good humor was restored.

They got onto an escalator to go down to the second level where Chap had spotted a shoe store. Chap and Catherine were side by side on one step with Peggy on the step below them.

Suddenly, a woman behind them screamed frantically, "He's got my purse!"

Instinctively, Chap reached down and snatched up Peggy to shield her. As Catherine whirled around to look behind her, a man violently shoved her out of his way. Chap heard the sickening thud of her head crashing into the side of the escalator, saw her body tumble down half a dozen steps. As the man leaped over her body, he flung out his arm which was carrying the stolen purse. In that split second, Chap saw the thin dirty-blonde braid that hung down the back of the black sleeveless tee shirt and the tattoo of a black snake—its thick black coils which encircled the man's pale upper arm, its slanted angry red eyes, and its forked red tongue.

The escalator continued its rumbling descent, carrying Catherine's crumpled body with her head pointed down. Her left arm was beneath her, but her right one was pointing toward the comb-like piece which seemed to be devouring the moving steps.

"Mommy, Mommy, Mommy," Peggy sobbed.

Clutching Peggy, Chap rushed down the moving steps.

"Help her!" he yelled.

Before Chap reached her, a muscular black man stepped from the crowd below and swept Catherine up into his arms a split second before her finger tips touched the teeth into which the stairs disappeared. Stepping away from the escalator, the man gently laid her down onto the floor.

"Oh, my god, thank you," Chap said breathlessly as he stepped off the escalator on legs that hardly seemed to support him. "I was afraid her hand—"

The man interrupted Chap with a quick, "You're welcome," before melting into the crowd of shoppers that was gathering.

Chapter 15

Chap stared down at his unmoving sister, her face as white as death as blood oozed from a gash in her forehead and trickled down beside her nose, under her eye, and across her temple like a dark red scar. The crowd standing around him was shrouded in a heavy fog that caused colors to swirl and muffled all sound, even the menacing growl of the escalator. Unable to move, with his feet frozen to the floor, Chap only stared as his heart pounded in his chest.

A man in a dark uniform stepped out of the crowd. Moving in slow motion, he flapped a pale blue blanket several time in the air before it settled down gently to cover Catherine's body. Then he knelt beside her. As he started to pull the blanket up, Chap tried to yell, "Not her face! You can't cover her face!" but no sound came out.

Suddenly, the crowd parted. A man in a tattered shirt stepped forward. His flushed face was contorted in an ugly grimace as he swung a bloody bat around and around his head. When Chap lunged forward to protect his sister, he crashed into the side of the hospital bed.

"Chap?" Catherine said weakly, her eyes blinking as she tried to focus on him.

"It's okay," he said, rising from the floor to caress the back of her hand. "Go back to sleep."

Her eyelids blinked—once, then twice more slowly—and she was asleep again.

Chap wiped the tears from his cheeks with the back of his shaking hand and sank back down onto the chair that was pulled up close to Catherine's bed, remembering bits and pieces of the nightmare as they faded from his memory—Catherine's blood like the scar on Erica's face, the blue blanket from the VA hospital in Illinois, Nelson Nelson and the bloody bat. . . . Chap massaged his left shoulder while slowly inhaling and exhaling to ease the pounding of his heart. Reaching down to the floor, he picked up the cotton blanket a nurse had given him and settled back into the chair, but sleep wouldn't come, not even as he listened to the hypnotically regular soft beeps of a monitor. From outside the room came the sounds of hushed voices and quiet footsteps and once the squeaky wheels of a gurney. In the semi-darkness of the room, he could see the huge clock on the wall. It was a few minutes before two o'clock Sunday morning.

Just a little over twelve hours ago, Peggy was trying to comprehend why her five-dollar bill wouldn't pay for a $4.95 book.

Just eleven hours ago, she'd been inconsolable in the waiting area of the emergency room until a nurse, who looked like a grandma should look, got her a cupcake and explained in language suitable for a seven-year-old what had happened to her mommy's wrist, what the doctor would do to fix it, and how the cast would look.

"You know," she said, "it won't be too long until not even Mommy will know her wrist was ever broken because the body is so good at healing."

Then, totally exhausted from fear and crying, Peggy had fallen asleep, curled up on Chap's lap. About thirty minutes after that, Lily and MayCee had come to take Peggy home with them. Chap thought that the words *very good friends* suited them much better than *roommates*.

Just ten hours ago, Chap had sat in the surgery waiting room with a police artist and a detective, Eric Cameron, describing not the purse snatcher's face, which he hadn't seen, but his braid and the snake tattoo.

Detective Cameron said, "The perp can cut his hair and change his clothes, but that tattoo is there forever!"

It was from the detective that Chap learned that the thief was suspected in eight other snatchings, but Catherine was the first person to be hurt. The detective also told Chap how lucky she was since a woman in Canada had fallen on an escalator and died when her scarf had gotten caught in the teeth at the bottom. The police were asking the man who'd saved Catherine to come forward.

Just nine hours ago, a young woman in a pair of dark green leggings covered with a flowing light-green, knee-length top, had approached him in the waiting room. Holding out her hand, she'd said, "I'm Madison Blaze, a social worker with the hospital. Detective Cameron tells me you've got some problems."

In short order, she got the pertinent information. There was no husband or boyfriend or parents or any other family members in San Diego to call, only Lori, a full continent away. Chap was supposed to return to Virginia in the morning. Catherine's car was still at Horton Plaza; Chap couldn't drive it. Catherine was employed as a teacher and thus had health insurance.

"It's my job to help people with problems related to hospitalizations, so let's tackle yours. I think you need to call your sister first. If you don't mind, I'd like to be on speaker phone so that I can help with the plans you have to make."

It felt like déjà vu—calling Lori with very bad news. Only this time, she was home and he was far away, not like before when she was in London and he was at home, trying to tell her that their father had almost frozen in the snow.

As soon as Lori heard his voice, she said, "Oh, Chap, I can't wait to hear all about what you three have been doing. I'm so envious, especially since it's about forty degrees here and ugly gray."

"Hello, Lori, I'm Madison Blaze, a hospital social worker. I'm on the speaker with Chap."

"Oh, my God—hospital? Are you all right? Catherine? Peggy?" There was fear in her voice.

"Catherine's hurt, but she'll be okay in time," Chap said.

Then he told her about the purse snatcher, the ride to the hospital, the surgery, and Catherine's prognosis.

Madison said, "My job is to help you and Chap. When Catherine is able, we'll talk with her also."

During the next fifteen minutes, Chap, Madison, and Lori made plans. Lori would cancel Chap's flight for the next day and book tickets for a trip out. Madison would contact Horton Plaza so that Catherine's car wouldn't be towed. Chap would call the Academy Monday morning to inform Miss Sydney that he wouldn't be back for a while. Then after Lori and Madison exchanged phone numbers, the call ended.

"Well, when we have time, I want to hear about this school where no one cares if you don't come back from spring break on time!" Madison said with a grin.

Chap smiled, remembering how strange it had once seemed to him.

Madison continued, "I'll check in with you and Catherine tomorrow. We'll need to see what all she had in her purse. I can help with canceling credit cards and stopping phone service on her cell."

"No need to do that. I have her purse."

"What do you mean?"

"He didn't steal my sister's purse. He knocked her down after he stole someone else's purse."

"My mistake! I assumed that since she was hurt by the purse snatcher that he also stole her purse. Well, that's one less worry for your sister. I'll come by tomorrow anyway to see if you've thought of anything else I can do for you."

Just eight hours ago, at six o'clock, Catherine's fall had made the evening news in Southern California since a reporter and camera man just happened to have stepped off the escalator when Catherine was assaulted. They were at Horton Plaza to interview a manager about an upcoming community event. They'd missed getting a shot of the fleeing thief, but they'd gotten pictures of Catherine on the floor, waiting for the ambulance, and of Peggy and Chap, too.

At the end of the segment, a police officer at the scene said, "We'd like the Good Samaritan who saved this young mother from further injury or even death to contact us. Perhaps he can help us solve this crime."

Chap saw the story on one of the four television sets in the huge surgery waiting room. He thought he'd looked really dumb on television—bug-eyed and pale—as he stammered into the mike which had been shoved in front of his face, "I'm Chap. She's my sister, Catherine. She lives here, but I'm just visiting from Indiana—I mean Virginia."

Like, duh, he didn't even know where he lived?

An elderly, white-haired lady sitting one seat down from him said, as she pointed toward the screen, "That young man looks a lot like you, dear. I guess it's true that everyone in the world has a double."

Chap started to explain that he was that young man, but the lady was already engrossed in the next news story.

Just seven hours ago, Chap had risen from his seat to meet the orthopedic surgeon, who briskly described, using lots of unfamiliar words to name various bones, what had been done to Catherine's shattered wrist. The gist of it was that her wrist was now held together with pins and encased in a heavy cast. A plastic surgeon on call had stitched the gash on her forehead. She had a mild concussion as well as multiple bruises on her body and her face.

At that point, Chap's face lost its color, and he swayed a bit. Suddenly, the surgeon did an un-surgeon like thing. He put his arm around Chap's shoulders and helped him to a seat nearby.

"How old are you?" he said as if seeing Chap for the first time.

"Seventeen."

"Oh, so you're not her husband."

"I'm her younger brother, visiting for a few days."

"I'm sorry. I should've noticed that you aren't the age of a husband. I shouldn't have been quite so blunt. I won't tell you that your sister wasn't badly injured because she was, but she will recover. It's going to take time—first several days here and then two or three weeks at home before she returns to work. After the pins are removed, she'll need therapy to regain wrist mobility. But I repeat, she will recover because she's young and healthy."

With that, he stood and shook Chap's hand. "I suppose I'll see you when I make my rounds. Any questions now?"

Chap only shook his head.

"Then I suggest you go get something to eat. If I remember right, seventeen-year-old guys are always hungry." He smiled. "The cafeteria quits serving supper at 8:00. The lady at the check-in desk will give you a pager in case you are needed back here. Otherwise, you have about an hour before your sister will be transferred from recovery to a room. Good evening."

Lori had called as Chap was finishing up a plate of meatloaf and mashed potatoes—the former rather dried out and the latter cold and lumpy. She told him when she and Doug would arrive in San Diego. She'd already canceled his return ticket for the next morning.

Just six hours ago, he'd followed the gurney from the recovery room to Room 605. Catherine had not awakened, only moaned, as she was transferred from the gurney to the bed. Then a parade of people in scrubs came and went for the next half an hour. Chap stood silently in one corner of the room, trying to stay out of the way, trying not to look at the unmoving body of his sister, trying not to let his mounting fears show.

Then he sat and sat on the hard, plastic-covered chair seat—staring at the nondescript walls of the room, watching the last bit of light fade behind the partially closed blinds, waiting for what he knew not.

He felt as if he were in the midst of a real, wide-awake nightmare with painfully familiar parts. His father lying in the snow, unresponsive. . . the green walls of the emergency room in Riverwoods. . . the VA hospital in Illinois where his father had taken his last breath. . . Lou Ella's blood creating an ever-widening stain on the beige carpet. . . Owen's broken arm. . . the EMTs. . . Detective Jarvek with all the questions. . . .

Only now it was Detective Cameron, not Detective Jarvek. It was Catherine's wrist that was broken, not Owen's arm. The criminal was not an old drunk, but a young thief. The hospital blanket covered not his silent father, but his unmoving sister.

* * *

Chap awakened at 6:30 when a nurse came in to check Lori's vitals. His neck was stiff from sleeping in the hard chair. He could only imagine how rumpled he must look. After asking the nurse what time the cafeteria opened for breakfast, he headed down to the men's room at the end of the long empty hallway. Splashing water on his face and running a comb through his hair did little to improve his appearance, but he felt better anyway.

Because he hadn't bought sandals for the three of them at Horton Plaza, he had plenty of money in his pocket. In the cafeteria, he filled a tray with a bowl of oatmeal, a plate of scrambled eggs and bacon, a dish of fresh fruit, and a raspberry Greek yogurt. Since it promised to be a long day of sitting in Catherine's room, he got a cup of coffee, which he didn't even like, but maybe it would help him stay awake.

When he returned to Catherine's room, she was just waking up again. Her face was very pale in contrast to the ugly bruises on her forehead and cheek. She was squinching up her eyes and then opening them wide.

"Everything's kind of blurry, almost like I'm seeing double," she said.

"That's because of the concussion."

"And my headache?"

"That, too."

"What else do you know?"

"Don't you want to ask the doctor yourself when he makes rounds?"

"I will, but I'd like to have some idea from you first."

"Okay," Chap said. "This is what I know. Your wrist is held together with pins. It will heal, but you'll need therapy later to make it mobile again. You have a concussion, so you'll be here a few days because of that. You have stitches in your forehead, but your curly bangs will cover the scar."

"The doctor said that?"

"No, I made that up."

When Catherine wrinkled up her nose at him, Chap relaxed a bit. His sister might look like she'd lost a boxing match, but her sense of humor was intact.

"Where's Peggy?"

"Home with Lily and MayCee. She'll be here later today after you've rested more."

Then Chap told her about talking to Detective Cameron and the sketch artist, about Madison Blaze's role in some plans, and about his cancelled flight. He decided not to tell her about Doug and Lori's flight plans. That would be a surprise.

"And I slept through all of that?"

"You did. You've been absolutely no help at all. Oh, but you did make the news last night."

"Oh, God, really?"

"A great shot of you lying on the floor, looking like an injured Snow White waiting for a handsome prince—or maybe just an EMT."

Catherine wrinkled up her nose again.

"Seriously, a man saved you from greater harm. He picked you up off the escalator so that you didn't get caught in the bottom part. The police have asked him to come forward in case he saw the thief."

At that moment, an aide entered to help Catherine order her breakfast. Moments later, the surgeon strode in to give his detailed explanation about the surgery and prognosis. Soon after he left, Madison Blaze arrived to meet Catherine and offer help. Then the floor doctor came to examine Catherine and to tell her about the effects of a concussion.

By ten o'clock, Catherine had finished some of her breakfast and had dozed off, exhausted from all the attention. Chap decided to take a walk around the hospital and possibly go outside—anything to keep himself awake. The coffee hadn't helped at all, and he'd drunk every single bitter, nasty drop.

As he approached the main entrance on the first floor, he spied an enclosed courtyard with several picnic tables and lots of flowers, probably a place employees used for breaks. No one was there at the time. Chap pushed open the glass door and entered. Suddenly, he seemed alone in the midst of a busy hospital and a bustling city. The high walls of the hospital that surrounded the area blocked all traffic sounds, and the glass walls on one side muted all hospital noise.

Chap sank down on one of the picnic benches and pulled his cell phone from his pocket. After calculating the time difference, he called Chicago. When no one answered, he left a message—Catherine had been hurt, and he would be staying in San Diego awhile longer.

There never seemed to be a time when he didn't wish Erica was with him to share whatever he was experiencing. He wondered how long it would be before he'd know if his dreams of being with her would come true. Did any guy ever end up with the girl he'd fallen in love with when he was fifteen?

After another walk around the hospital and a quick stop for a second cup of coffee and a cinnamon roll, Chap skipped an elevator ride and trudged up the six flights in the dingy stairwell with rough gray concrete walls and dim lighting. At the top, however, he felt winded rather than invigorated. As he approached the nearby elevator doors, one pinged and opened. Chap almost collided with Lori and Doug.

No one spoke. As they hugged, Chap relaxed. Lori was here. Now everything would be all right.

"Is there somewhere we can talk a bit before we see Catherine?" Lori asked.

"There's a waiting room just down the hall."

Once they were settled in chairs, Chap began to fill them in with all the details about the last twenty-four hours. It was a long story—the purse snatcher, the horrendous fall, the Good Samaritan, the police detective, the artist who drew the ugly black snake tattoo, the surgery, the concussion, the prognosis for Catherine's recovery. . . .

Apparently, Chap looked as tired and rumpled as he felt because when he finished answering all their questions, Lori said, "How about we all go see Catherine for a bit? Then I'll stay with her while you and Doug drive to the house for a rest and maybe a shower."

It was Chap's turn to wrinkle up his nose up at his sister. "Just because I slept in a chair for hours doesn't mean I look that bad!"

"I didn't say you looked that bad," she said with lots of emphasis on *looked* and a mischievous grin on her face.

"I get it. You don't have to get so personal. I'll take a shower."

"And I'll take one, too, before you start in on me!" Doug said.

"Then you can bring Peggy back with you. I called the house when we landed. Both Lily and MayCee have plans for the evening, which they are willing to cancel—they sound like really nice women—but I told them we'll take care of Peggy tonight."

"What about Catherine's car?" Chap asked.

"Already taken care of," said Doug. "Lily found Catherine's other set of keys. They drove to Horton's Plaza and got the car."

"You're right. They're very nice," Chap said.

* * *

When they entered Catherine's room, Chap realized what a shock her appearance must be to those seeing her for the first time. The bruise on her upper cheek was now a deep reddish-purple and her eye was both black and bloodshot. Her right arm was also bruised. The cast and the bandage on her forehead added to the dismal portrait.

Lori gasped. Doug's fingers on her shoulders tightened.

Catherine's eyes filled with tears. "I knew you'd come," she said with a catch in her voice." Then, smiling weakly, she added, "No one's let me have a mirror yet, but I don't suppose I look so good, do I?"

Lori laughed softly. "Well, I wouldn't enter a beauty contest right now if I were you, but let's not talk about how we look since Doug and I have spent the past twelve hours on planes and in airports."

Catherine's eyes filled with tears again. "I'm so glad you are all here. What would I've done if I'd been alone?"

"Well, you aren't alone, so don't even think about that," Lori said. "We'll help you get everything figured out."

Chap smiled as he looked at his sisters.

Chapter 16

The shower felt wonderful, but when Chap lay down for a short nap, sleep eluded him. After a while, he got up and found some lined paper.

March 31

Dear Erica,

I know I told you last night when you called all about what happened to Catherine. Lori and Doug arrived a few hours ago. It's a relief to know that they will take care of everything now. I keep getting into these situations where I'm supposed to know what to do, and I seem to do something, but I never know if what I do is right.

The floor doctor thinks Catherine can go home day after tomorrow if she does all right as they begin to wean her off the pain medication which is now in the IV. She'll have pills at home.

She'll need help for a while since she still has some double vision even though it's getting better, she says. She'll have to learn to do lots of things with only one hand until the heavy cast comes off and she gets a lighter brace. Though no one has yet mentioned me staying here for a few weeks, I know that's a possibility. Who else is there to help her? The roommates have been wonderful, but they have jobs—Lori and Doug, too. I don't, and I truly don't have to go back to school right away. Since I started at the Academy in the summer, I've already gone more than the required number of days for a school year.

I won't say this aloud to anyone, but I keep hoping there's another solution. I do care about Catherine and Peggy, but we're still getting to know each other. A weekend together last fall when Lori and Doug got married and barely five days here hardly make up for years of not knowing them at all. The idea of living with people I hardly know, as well as the two roommates, makes me feel uneasy. But then I feel guilty for even having that feeling. Does this make any sense?

Since I won't admit any of this to anyone else, it's possible that when I write again, my new address may be in San Diego for a while—but I hope not.

I miss you more than you can know.

With all my love, Chap

* * *

As Chap was writing Erica's address on the envelope, Peggy dashed into the house with Lily, who'd taken her to the park to distract her from her worries about her mother. Peggy had been so distraught the night before that Lily had finally slept in Catherine's bed so as to be close to her.

"Uncle Douglas!" she squealed. "Now I have two uncles here!"

"You can call me Uncle Doug if you'd like."

Peggy wrinkled up her nose. Chap sure knew where she'd gotten that mannerism.

"Uncle Doug?" She paused as she considered this change. Then she beamed and said, "All right, if you say so."

After a quick late lunch of what Peggy called her "recipe," which was celery stuffed with peanut butter and raisins, and a bologna sandwich, which was Chap's favorite, and more fresh-squeezed orange juice, the three of them got into the Toyota that Doug had rented at the airport and headed back to the hospital. As Doug drove, Chap helped prepare Peggy for what she would see—her mother's bruised face, her bandaged forehead, and the cast on her arm. Peggy's solemn eyes indicated that she understood. At least, Chap hoped so.

* * *

When they got off the elevator on the sixth floor, Peggy skipped down the long shiny tiled hallway ahead of Chap and Doug, her short braids bouncing with every step. Then she stopped and skipped back, pulling on their hands to make them walk faster.

At Room 605, Peggy whispered as she pushed the door open, "I have to be quiet now."

Catherine and Lori were both sleeping. Peggy put her fingers to her lips and tiptoed closer to her mother's bed. Then she froze, her eyes glued on a third woman who was standing away from the bed.

"Mommy," she said, forgetting to be quiet as she looked at the bed. "Aunt Lori," she said with assurance as she looked at the chair. Then, turning back to the woman, she said, with a frown on her face and her arms akimbo, "But who are *you*?"

Both Catherine and Lori awakened quickly. After glancing at Peggy, their eyes followed hers to the dark-haired, dark-eyed stranger standing quietly in the corner.

Suddenly, Catherine and Lori yelled together, "Marilee!"

Chap and Doug only stared from the doorway.

After a flurry of hugs, the sisters began to talk—one or two or three at a time. Peggy climbed up on the foot of the bed. Her little head swiveled all around as she listened to her mother and her two aunts who looked so much alike.

Catherine and Lori fired the questions—"How did you find us?" "When did you get here?" "Where do you live?"

As Chap and Doug listened, the story about what had led up to this family reunion in a hospital room unfolded. Marilee had seen the news story on the big television in the restaurant north of San Diego where she'd been working for the past few years. She immediately thought she recognized Catherine, lying on the floor in a pool of blood, and Chap's name was familiar although the pale young man on television didn't look at all like the brother she'd last seen when he was seven and a half. She had little hope of finding her brother and sister—if they were, in fact, her brother and sister—at one of the many hospitals in San Diego, but she asked her boss for time away from work anyway and headed south.

Actually, finding them had been much easier than she'd expected. She'd started at the police station closest to Horton Plaza. After conversations with several officers at the front desk, she finally got to see Detective Cameron, who'd pulled weekend duty. Because Marilee looked so much like Catherine, whom he'd interviewed briefly just that morning at the hospital, he accepted Marliee's claim to be her sister and told her where Chap and Catherine were.

Then Marilee asked the questions, and Lori and Catherine answered. Her last one, "How's Dad?" brought tears to their eyes.

"All right. Somebody needs to fill me in," Doug said quietly to Chap.

"Marilee ran away from home about ten years ago. She used to send postcards once in a while, but we never had an address for her, just the California post mark."

"I remember Lori mentioning that after your father's will was read. And you recognized her after all these years?"

"Wouldn't you? Just look at her," Chap said.

Marilee was an inch taller than Lori and Catherine who were both five foot two, but she was shorter than Julianna, who at five feet five had been called "the Smith giant." Marilee also had dark brown eyes and hair, but her hair was more wavy than curly. It hung rather limp to her shoulders. She had the dimples in both cheeks when she smiled like Lori had, but her skin lacked a healthy glow. She shared her sisters' oval face shape, but her cheek bones were more pronounced like Julianna's. She talked with her hands like her sisters did.

Doug grinned. "I see what you mean."

Finally, Marilee walked over to Chap and Doug and said, with the same mischievous grin that her sisters had, "So this is my little brother."

"Be careful," Lori said. "He can get testy when you add the 'little' part."

It was Chap's turn to wrinkle his nose up at her.

"And you must be a boyfriend or a husband," she said to Doug, extending a hand.

"I'm your brother-in-law since I just married Lori, so I deserve a hug instead of a handshake."

Then, turning to Chap, he said, "If those three chattered like they just did when you were little, it's a wonder you ever learned to talk at all since getting a word in edgewise would've been next to impossible!"

Chap could only smile when all three sisters wrinkled up their noses at Doug.

Peggy gave a big yawn and lay down on her mother's bed. In the way that yawns are infectious, Catherine also yawned.

"Looks like we all need to get some sleep. Besides that, we're breaking all sorts of hospital rules about how many visitors should be in a room at once," Catherine said with a smile. "I'm doing fine. Now go and get some sleep. I'll see you tomorrow."

In short order, it was decided that Doug, Lori, Chap, and Peggy would go back to the house. Lori and Doug would sleep on the living room pullout, and Chap would sleep in Catherine's bed. Marilee had a room in a motel nearby. They'd visit in shifts the next day so as not to wear Catherine out.

After a lot more hugs, everyone left the hospital.

* * *

Chap woke up early since his body was still on Eastern time. Peggy was snuggled down in her little trundle bed with only her dark hair showing from beneath the blankets. Chap tiptoed to the bathroom first and then to the kitchen where MayCee was having toast and coffee. Whispering, she told him that she planned to see Catherine before she went to work. She asked if he wanted a ride.

Thirty minutes later, Chap, showered and dressed, wrote a note to Lori and Doug, telling them that he was going to the hospital with MayCee. Then, a banana in hand, he climbed into the front seat of her Jeep. As she expertly maneuvered through rush hour traffic on the freeway, she got bits and pieces of the life stories of the rest of the Smith family.

"You all have quite a history, which makes my upbringing in a San Diego suburb with two parents and no siblings seem terribly ordinary. Even my job is ordinary. I sit at a computer all day, entering data."

"Well, less than two years ago, I thought my life was very ordinary. Lori, my father, and I had a very set routine. My life was predictable, and I was content. Then Lori got a temporary job transfer to Virginia, and I was home with just my father. Everything went to hell in a handbasket."

"Do you know where that expression 'to hell in a handbasket' came from—according to my grandma, that is?" MayCee asked.

"No. I've just heard people use it."

"Ready for something gruesome?"

"Yes."

"Well, years ago, when people were executed by a guillotine, their heads were carted away in a basket. Because they were supposedly criminals, they were going to hell. Get it—went to hell in a handbasket?"

Chap grimaced. "Got it. Guess I won't use that expression again."

MayCee laughed as she parked in the visitors' lot. Then she and Chap entered the hospital and rode up to the sixth floor. Catherine was sitting up in bed, still looking bruised and battered but more alert. Her breakfast tray was almost empty.

"Hey, I'm glad to see some familiar faces," she said.

"Since we're in a hospital, I think the response to that is supposed to be something like 'You're looking good this morning,' but I can't quite manage that," said MayCee with a grin. "You're still quite colorful, and you could use a comb and brush."

"Well, Chap," Catherine said, "has MayCee shown you her brutally honest side yet?"

"No, she's been nice to me."

Everyone laughed.

Then Chap listened as MayCee and Catherine made some plans about getting Peggy to and from school, paying some of the shared bills, and figuring out how much Lily and MayCee could help when Catherine got home.

As MayCee was leaving, Marliee entered.

"You must be the long-lost sister. Wow, you three really do look a lot alike."

"So we hear. That makes it hard for us to argue about who's the ugliest," Marilee said.

Chap smiled. He thought he was going to like this sister, too.

* * *

When Catherine began to look tired, Marilee and Chap left for a late breakfast in the cafeteria. Away from the dim lighting in the hospital room, Chap looked more carefully at this new sister. She certainly did resemble the other three, but there was a sort of tiredness about her. Her skin was not quite so young looking, her hair was a bit duller, and her eyes were more shadowed.

Struggling, as he so often did, with what he could say to this almost stranger, he said what first popped into his mind.

"So you're older than Lori but younger than Catherine and Julianna."

"That's true, but you're wondering why I look older than all of them."

Chap felt the heat move into his face.

Marilee smiled gently. "Don't be embarrassed. I didn't follow a very healthy lifestyle for a lot of years."

Without thinking, Chap said, "What did you do?"

Then, realizing that he was asking what she might not want to answer, he hurriedly added, "Not that you need to tell me."

"That's okay. I'm not proud of most of my past. Even so, I don't intend to hide it from all of you either. Actually, I've wanted to go back to Indiana for several years, but I didn't have the guts to face you all and Dad. I'm thrilled to have found you now.

"I couldn't believe it when I saw that news clip on TV. I realized that maybe fate was telling me that it was time to make the changes I've been thinking about for a long time."

Marilee paused to focus on the huge cinnamon roll in front of her.

Finally, Chap said, "What kind of changes?"

"Well, for one thing, I never graduated from high school."

"You didn't?"

"Nope."

"What have you been doing?"

"Well, that's the problem because I mostly did bad things for a long time."

Chap didn't know how to respond to that at all, so he just concentrated on the scrambled eggs and toast in front of him.

Marilee continued. "It didn't take me long to figure out that I wasn't going to become a movie star. I wasn't that stupid, but I tried to hang around where the stars were. I got a few menial jobs at a television studio—mostly office work, even some cleaning. I met a few influential people, got invited to a few parties, started drinking and smoking marijuana—lying to myself that I could handle it, that I wouldn't have problems like others had.

"Well, guess what? I wasn't any smarter than anyone else. Within a few years, I was rarely sober, unemployed, sleeping on any sofa I could find, and believing that those helping me find marijuana and alcohol were my friends.

"Then I met this really nice guy, Chance. He helped me get a job as a waitress in a nice restaurant, and pretty soon I was living with him in a fancy apartment in Hollywood. Chance didn't use drugs, but he drank. I followed his lead. I quit smoking marijuana, but I continued to drink a lot.

"Then, one day, a knock on the door changed everything. It turned out Chance didn't *use* drugs, but he *sold* them—lots of them—to college kids mostly. A raid on the apartment found over $20,000 worth of pills and a gym bag full of cash. We were arrested and charged with felonies. I spent about five months in jail and detoxed the hard way. Before the trial, Chance surprisingly did a very decent thing. He told the prosecutor that I had no knowledge of any drugs. Luckily, she believed him, mostly because I had no prior arrests."

By this time, Chap was only staring at this sister. Her eyes were so sad.

"When I got released, I joined AA. Some truly good people at the meetings helped me make the decision to leave Los Angeles and the life and people I'd known there. I ended up in San Diego County, where I've lived for the past three years. I've been working as a waitress, going to AA meetings, and staring at the walls of my dumpy, little, nondescript apartment. Mostly, I've been trying not to slide back into that other life, but lots of times recently, I've wondered why I even try to live a sober life since it's been absolutely no fun and not very rewarding. Then I saw you and Catherine on television."

Tears welled up in her eyes. Chap was silent.

"Do you believe in signs?"

"I don't know. I don't think I've ever looked for one."

"Well, I think you all are a sign that I'm supposed to go back home and do what I probably would've done if I hadn't run away years ago."

"You mean finish school."

"Yes, but even before that, I need to figure out how I'm supposed to fit into this world," Marilee said. "I need a purpose."

"You know you have some money."

"What money?"

"The inheritance from our father."

"I was still in the will?" Marilee said, her eyes wide and her eyebrows raised.

"Your share was to be kept for five years from the date of our father's death and then split up four ways if we didn't hear from you. Lori can explain it all."

Now the tears were sliding down her cheeks. She rummaged around in her purse to find a packet of tissues.

Finally, she said, "I was just too much of a coward to face Dad. He didn't deserve what I did to him."

Neither one spoke as they finished eating their breakfasts.

"You know we don't live in Indiana anymore," Chap said as he put their dirty dishes onto the cafeteria trays. "The house was sold after our father went to the VA hospital in Illinois. Lori needed to go back to her new job in Virginia, and Doug was there."

"How has this been for you—leaving Riverwoods, I mean?"

"I guess I realized that when the changes started coming so fast that I had no choice but to go along with them. I was just sixteen."

"How's city life?"

"Not my favorite at all. I think I'm still a country kid by nature, but I'm in a great experimental school called the Academy for Mutual Instruction."

Marilee looked at her watch. "Let's leave that for our next talk. We probably need to get back up to see Catherine now. I still haven't heard what she's been doing since she left home. Well, I know part of what she's been doing since she has Peggy. Isn't she a cutie?" Marilee smiled and added, "How did they end up in San Diego? I thought she was in Portland."

Chap grinned. "That's quite a story. I'll let her tell you when she's up to it."

Chapter 17

When Chap and Marilee got to Room 605, the door was ajar. Chap was about to push it open when the voice inside caught his attention. Putting his finger to his lips, he motioned for Marilee to come closer.

"Catherine, I was so shocked to see you on television. I had no idea you were in San Diego. Are you just visiting here?"

They didn't hear Catherine's response.

The man continued. "I know you were very angry to find out about my wife—"

"And kids!" This time Catherine's voice was very clear.

"Yes, I have two children I love dearly, but the minute I saw you at that party, I knew we were soul mates. I've thought of you every day all these months. I've been desperate since you disappeared from Portland. Catherine, I've never loved anyone as I love you. I'll provide an apartment for you and Peggy here in San Diego so we can be together even more often than we used to be."

"You'll fake more business trips?" Catherine asked.

Chap's heart fell. Catherine was going to let this man back into her life.

"Something like that. My wife knows I have to be gone a lot. Please say yes."

Chap wondered if the man was on his knees by Catherine's bedside. The silence inside the room got very long.

Finally, Catherine spoke, definitely loud enough for Chap and Marilee to hear. "I'm still young and not too hard on the eyes. I have a beautiful, funny daughter. I have a college education and a career I love. Someday I will be a good catch for a man who wants us. That won't be you, Bryan, because"—her voice rose many decibels—"*you are married, you son of a bitch.*"

As if that were their cue to enter, Chap and Marilee stepped into the drama.

Speaking quietly now, Catherine said, "I don't think you've ever met my brother and sister, Chap and Marilee." Then looking at them, she said, "This is Bryan. He's leaving now."

"But Catherine, I want you—"

Quickly, Chap walked up to the man and said, "But Catherine *doesn't* want you."

Bryan looked up at Chap, who was inches taller, twenty pounds of muscle heavier, and ready to protect his sister. After a long look at Catherine, Bryan turned and left the room.

"Oh, my, there must be a good story here," Marilee said.

"Not worth hearing."

"Like I'm going to believe that. I've told Chap about some of my sordid background, which I'll tell you. But first, tell me about Bryan, the son—"

Catherine interrupted. "You don't have to say it. I'm trying to clean up my language."

Marilee's face became softer. "I don't mean to pry. It's just that I've found my family again, and I want you to accept me even with all my dirty laundry. Shouldn't we be honest with each other?"

Tears welled up in Catherine's eyes. Motioning to both Chap and Marilee, she held out her left hand. "Peggy has had only me since she was born. Now she's met three aunts and two uncles. We have a true family. I intend for that to mean more than an occasional letter, call, or visit, so the answer is yes. Real families are honest. They help each other. They laugh and cry together. I want all of that."

Catherine snatched a tissue from the box on the table by her bed, dabbed at her eyes, and unceremoniously blew her nose.

Then, looking at both of them, she said with a mischievous smile, "But right now, I'd rather laugh than cry."

Marilee grinned. "Okay by me, so who's going to tell the first knock-knock joke?"

Chap sank down onto a chair by the bed and groaned loudly as his sisters told one bad joke after another.

* * *

Everyone was in the room—Marilee, Doug, Lori, and Chap—waiting for Catherine's release papers to arrive. Catherine was dressed in black slacks and a loose blue shirt that fit over her cast. The dark purple bruises on her face and body were now tinged with green. A brush had helped her tousled hair, but overall, except for the wide grin on her face, Catherine still looked pretty badly beaten up.

When there was a light knock on the door, everyone turned, expecting to see someone with the discharge papers in hand. Instead, what they saw was a huge colorful bouquet of spring flowers with a pair of skinny legs beneath it. The head of a teenager poked out from around the flowers.

"Catherine Smith?" the young man asked.

"I'm Catherine."

"Then these are for you."

"Are you sure? I don't know anyone who'd send me flowers."

"Well, Ma'am, you do now."

With that comment, he placed the bouquet on the table beside Catherine's bed and left.

"Wow, that's some bunch of flowers," Marilee said. "Who are they from?"

Turning the bouquet around, Lori found the card stuck inside and handed it to Catherine.

"Throw those flowers in the trash!" Catherine yelled as she pitched the card onto the floor. "That son—"

She paused, relaxing her angry face a bit. Then, taking a deep breath, she said in a much lower tone, "Please throw those flowers away."

"Oh, come on, Catherine. Let's enjoy them," said Lori. "There are daffodils and tulips in the bouquet. You can't know how much we look forward to spring flowers in a drab city that's been brown and gray all winter."

The stormy look on Catherine's face faded, replaced with a slight smile that played at the corner of her lips.

"Oh, boy, I remember that look. What are you going to do?" Marilee said with raised eyebrows.

At that moment, a nurse entered the room. "Well, it looks like you've been sprung!" she said.

She went over the instructions for Catherine's home care in detail. Then an elderly male volunteer with a wheelchair arrived. Chap picked up Catherine's belongings that were in a large plastic bag with the hospital logo on the side, and the entourage slowly left the room and headed for the elevators. Marilee carried the flower bouquet, which she would transport in her car.

When Catherine was wheeled out through the main entrance, she was met by a female news reporter and a camera man. Immediately, her hand flew up to her disheveled hair as she said, "Oh, no."

Before she could protest any further, Detective Cameron and the black man whom Chap recognized from Horton Plaza stepped forward.

"Catherine, this is Carter Alexander. He's the man who picked you up off the escalator and kept you from experiencing further injury."

Carter nodded his head toward Catherine, looking as if he'd prefer to be anywhere else in the world besides in front of a camera.

"Just did what needed to be done like anyone would've," he said in a deep, musical voice.

Except that no one else had reacted to get Catherine off that escalator, Chap thought.

The reporter asked them all to stand behind Catherine while she shook hands with Carter Alexander. As the camera man filmed, the reporter said, "Now, there's another whole part to this story."

Then she explained how Marilee had found her long-lost brother and two sisters.

Shoving the microphone in front of Chap's red face, she asked, "How old were you when you last saw your sister?"

"Seven."

"How do you feel about meeting her again?"

"Good."

There was a pause while the reporter waited for Chap to say more. When he didn't, she mercifully moved on to talk more with his sisters.

Oh, God, Chap thought. I probably looked like a total idiot again, and this time I said only two words.

As the news reporter was wrapping up the segment, there were lots of hugs all around and not only for the camera. Then, finally, they were in the car and headed home.

* * *

After Catherine was comfortably settled on the couch with the flowers prominently displayed on the coffee table in front of her, she said, "I need a note card and my address book which are in the top right drawer of my dresser."

With those items in hand, she batted her eyelids in a flirty manner and looked at the ceiling as if contemplating her next words carefully. Then, in a syrupy sweet voice, she said, "Dear Bryan, I have received the lovely flowers you sent. I'm sure that you know how I feel about them. Catherine."

"How's that?" she said in a matter-of-face tone, turning to look at everyone.

"You're going to send a note like that to his house?" Lori asked, her eyebrows raised.

"Yes, I am."

"Ooh, you are devious," Marliee said with a grin. "I love it."

"And I'm not even done," said Catherine. "I still have the engagement ring."

"What are you going to do with it?" asked Lori.

"Don't you think his poor wife would enjoy a surprise gift?"

This time everyone said, "Oooooooh."

Thirty minutes later, the un-thank-you note for the flowers was in the mailbox, ready to be picked up, and the diamond ring was in its blue velvet box which was nestled in bubble wrap inside a small cardboard mailer. With it was a second note, carefully typed by Lori. *"My darling, I don't think I tell you often enough how much I love you. You are a wonderful wife and mother. Please enjoy this diamond which will represent my love forever. Bryan."*

The ring would be mailed at the end of the week.

Chapter 18

Chap stared out the small window as the plane lifted off the ground. His heart thudded as it flew west over the Pacific Ocean. Huge navy ships in the San Diego Harbor appeared to get smaller and smaller. Fishing boats farther out looked miniscule. Then the plane began a gentle 180-degree turn back east. Chap settled into his seat as the city disappeared beneath the clouds. In the middle seat, Lori snuggled up to Doug, her head on his shoulder. Chap was going home. All three of them were going home.

Chap pulled some paper out of the book he'd carried onto the plane.

April 6

Dear Erica,

I'm on my way back to Virginia—Lori and Doug, too. It's hard to know where to start telling you about all that has happened in the past week. Catherine was released from the hospital as scheduled. Her double vision is almost gone. It bothers her mostly when she's tired. She still can't read or watch TV much or the headache returns. Peggy is thrilled to have her home.

I know I was worried about staying to help out, but I offered anyway. You won't believe what happened instead.

Marilee informed us that she'd called her boss at the restaurant. She informed him that she hadn't taken vacation time in three years and that she needed it all now. She must be some terrific waitress because he agreed. She'll stay with Catherine and Peggy for at least three weeks. Hopefully, by then, Catherine will need so little help that Lily and MayCee can fill in. I'm still amazed that those three ladies are such good friends since their only connection is that they share a house in a city where rents are so high that having your own place is often impossible. Sure boosts one's opinion of the human race!

Catherine made the news again when she left the hospital. Her fall on the escalator and near escape of having her hand or hair get caught in the comb part at the bottom was one thing. Then there was the hero who rescued her. Finally, when Detective Cameron came by the hospital again, he found out about our reunion with Marilee. He hadn't realized when he first met Marilee that she hadn't seen any of us for ten years.

When we left the hospital Tuesday afternoon, a news crew was there with Detective Cameron and the man who'd saved Catherine. Carter Alexander is an elementary teacher like Catherine with a wife and three little boys. He said he's never done anything even remotely heroic before. He just acted without thinking. There were lots of hugs and handshakes. Then Marilee's story was covered—how she'd seen the newscast and found us. So that was our fifteen minutes of fame in Southern California.

We spent the last few days doing whatever we could to help Catherine and Peggy—the roommates, too. We thoroughly cleaned Catherine and Peggy's room, stripped their beds, and got all the laundry done. Then we washed the windows in the whole house and scrubbed down the patio. Lori cooked several big meals for all of us, including Lily and MayCee, and then froze leftovers for extra meals later. Doug and I even did some weeding and trimming in the tiny yard.

It was hard to leave this whole new family of mine. Lori didn't even try to hold back her tears. Maybe it's because we don't have living parents or grandparents that we feel so close.

Since today is Saturday, I'll have tomorrow to get unpacked and laundry done before I go back to school on Monday. By the way, I did get to tell that social worker, Madison Blaze, about the Academy. She came by a time or two to meet Lori and the rest of the group. Nice lady. She claims that her dream is to become part of a school system. She thinks the Academy sounds wonderful. I gave her Miss Sydney's name and email address since I know there's a regular parade of people who come through the school to observe it. I'm sure ready to go back.

This last little bit of news is more a hope than news. I think I told you that Doug has expressed interest in moving away from a big metropolitan area like DC. I know Lori loved country-small city living. Anyway, Marilee definitely wants to leave California, and Catherine has no real reason to stay there. She even told me about wanting to live in a place more like Riverwoods. I think there's a chance—just a chance—that they all might relocate back in the Midwest where they'd be closer to each other. Besides, Julianna is already there. As you can imagine, she has received a bunch of phone calls—first about the accident and then about Marilee finding us. So hope with me—cross your fingers— do whatever it takes to get us back "home."

Loving you always, Chap

P.S. I won't be close to you at O'Hare this time. This flight goes through Denver.

* * *

When Chap walked into the Language Arts Center on Monday morning, De and Owen, both grinning broadly, held up a banner which said, "Welcum bak, Chap," each letter a different color.

As they ate peanut butter cookies Miss April had baked in honor of Chap's return, De said, "I made that sign myself, just for you."

"It's a beautiful sign, De. I'm really glad to be back."

And he was.

* * *

By the end of the day, Chap was back in his Academy routine. At home, he, Doug, and Lori settled into their quiet, comfortable evenings together. Except for the frequent phone calls to and from their sisters, life was back to normal. Lori was thrilled when their yard burst into bloom with not only daffodils but also hyacinths and tulips of every color. First, three big shaggy forsythia bushes bloomed, then two flowering crab trees were covered in deep-pink blossoms, and finally, a lilac shrub scented the entire yard. Chap got out the mower, gassed it up, and began his weekly task of keeping the grass cut. And so April faded into May and May into June.

* * *

Journal Entry #11 - June 1

I know it's been a while since I sent a journal entry to you. I think it was right after I got home from California. Not quite a year has passed since Lori and I arrived at the apartment complex. What a year it's been!

Anyway, life did finally settle back down after the fun, exciting, scary, difficult, worrisome—I'm practicing my adjective use—time in San Diego. By the way, the purse snatcher has been caught. He was actually tackled by a couple of teen-agers right after he snatched another purse a week later in a different San Diego mall. Detective Cameron believes he'll get a hefty sentence since he'll be charged with assault, not just theft. Catherine will likely have to testify unless he pleads guilty.

By mid-April, Catherine was back with her group of happy little second graders, who decorated the classroom the day before she returned with homemade banners and streamers. She's healing well. Her heavy cast is off, the pins are out, and she's in therapy.

Marilee's story is a big one also. While she was staying with Catherine, she completely fell in love with her little niece which has led to her desire to work with kids. She's now determined to get her GED first and then start classwork for at least an associate's degree in early child education.

I guess she and Catherine talked for hours since both are planning to leave California for sure. It was Catherine's idea to look into Illinois rather than Indiana for several reasons. First, it's closer to Julianna in Missouri. In addition, it has an extensive community college system where non-traditional students, like Marilee, have lots of options for class work, and, of course, there are some major universities as well. Finally, there are many small and middle-sized cities across the center of the state with lots of small towns surrounding them, not to mention three big cities close enough for weekend excursions—St. Louis, Chicago, and Indianapolis.

With both Catherine and Marilee looking into moving to Illinois, Lori and Doug have begun to talk more seriously about relocating also. I made it clear from the first mention of moving that I was for it! This city boy would love to be a country or at least a smaller-city boy again.

As always, thanks for the ear.

P.S. I think "ear" is a bad metaphor for an email, but who would ever say, "Thanks for the eye"?

* * *

With June came suffocating heat and humidity. Chap mowed the yard as close to dark as he could after spraying himself with mosquito repellent, but he was still drenched in sweat by the time he finished. The air at the bus stop was heavy and stinky with vehicle fumes, but, at least, the Academy was cool inside.

Chap again longed for the green Indiana woods and Wandering River, which would be gurgling among the rocks beneath the wooden bridge. He wondered if the heron was back from its southern migration.

When the phone rang on June 3rd, Chap answered.

"Hey, Chap, it's Julianna."

"Are you okay?"

Julianna laughed. "Are you so traumatized that you assume that every phone call is bad news?"

"No, I'm *not* so traumatized. You just usually call in the evening when Lori is home."

"True. But I have news I just can't keep. Don't worry. It's good news."

"I'm going to get to hear it first?"

"You bet. Actually, it's news in two parts. First, Greg and I are getting married on August 1st. It'll be a small wedding with family and a few friends."

"Congratulations! We've been expecting to hear this news."

"Will you walk me down the aisle?"

Chap hesitated, trying not to picture wearing a suit or, even worse, a tuxedo in August in the Midwest. The silence got long.

"Chap, did you hear me? Will you walk me down the aisle?"

"I guess so," he said without enthusiasm.

"I detect a problem. What is it?"

"Will I have to wear a tuxedo?" he blurted out.

"So that's it!" Julianna said with a laugh. "No, you won't have to wear a tux. How about just slacks and a short-sleeved shirt?"

"Fine," Chap said, this time with enthusiasm. "So what's part two?"

"Our getting married may not have surprised you, but I'll bet this next bit will." Julianna stopped talking.

"Okay, drama queen, what's the news? I'm sufficiently curious now."

Julianna laughed again before she continued. "I know that Marilee and Catherine are looking into moving to Illinois. Well, Greg has accepted a job teaching graphic design at a liberal arts college in Prairie City, starting in early September. That's Prairie City, Illinois! Can you believe that coincidence? That leaves just the three of you to get your act together and move there also. I don't think it's against the laws of man or nature for Hoosiers to become Illinoisans—God, that's an awkward word!"

Chap laughed.

"I've got to go. Have Lori call me Saturday when we'll have time to really talk."

Chap's heart was pounding as he hung up the phone.

* * *

June 23

Dear Erica,

IT'S HAPPENING! I intentionally haven't called or written until I had real news, not just hopes. I hardly know where to start.

First, it was Marilee. Like I told you before, after she went back to her place, which she called "a dumpy, little, nondescript apartment," she became even more determined to leave California. When Julianna called her about their upcoming marriage and move to Illinois, Marilee went into high gear and hit the jackpot right away. Using craigslist, she found an ad for a furnished room to rent in a little house in the country. The owner, a retired music teacher, does organic vegetable gardening for local farmers' markets, raises chickens for eggs, and teaches piano lessons. The best part is that the house is about fifteen miles from a community college.

After a lot of phone calls and texts with pictures, Marilee sent the first month's rent without even seeing the house or meeting the lady! Then she drove across country by herself in her little red Ford. She moved in a week ago. The first reports from the "farm," as she calls it, are glowing. She likes the lady even though she is a bit eccentric. She eats only organic food— mostly salads with umpteen veggies in them, has a beautiful but unfriendly cat named Mozart, owns thousands of books which fill large bookcases in her small house, and has no television. Marilee is helping with some gardening in exchange for piano lessons! Can you believe that?? She has found a part-time waitress job at a family restaurant, and she is already enrolled in GED classes at the community college for the fall session. In the pictures she has sent from Illinois, she looks so happy, even healthier already—or do I just want to think that?

Meanwhile, Catherine has found out what she'll need to do to get an Illinois teaching certificate. It's doable, she says. Here's the real surprise. Marilee's landlady's sister lives about ten miles away. She and her husband have a studio apartment above a garage-workshop they added to the back of their old farmhouse about twenty years ago. Their current tenant is getting married at the end of June, so they're looking for a new renter. Marilee has been over to see the place. She says it's very cute with sloping ceilings and lots of window. The appliances are all furnished.

Catherine, however, feels the need to plan very carefully before moving because Peggy will be affected, too, so they're flying to Illinois tomorrow for a visit. According to Catherine's last phone call, her list of questions she needs answers for is already up to nineteen. It seems to me that impulsively running off with John and then moving to San

Diego to be with Bryan have made her overly cautious about moving in general!

That leads me to Lori and Doug. The talk around here is more and more related to moving to Illinois. The question now isn't if they'll move but when. Lori wants to go back to college part-time to get a bachelor's degree—maybe in nursing, she says. Doug likes office work a lot more than she does, so he'll likely stay in his line of work, especially since he already has a college degree in computer technology.

Even though they aren't saying so, there is one big problem now—ME! I can't finish enough course work to earn a high school diploma from the Academy until at least the end of this year and more likely next spring. I don't want to hold them back from moving, but at the same time, I don't want to leave the Academy yet. WHAT SHOULD I DO?

Enough about me and my siblings! Are you enjoying your summer job at the high school? If you are helping with some of the inside cleaning and outside landscaping work, I assume your leg is strong again. I'm glad about that.

I shared your story about your "naughty grandma" with Lori and Doug—how when she's feeling "naughty," she licks her knife unless she thinks the neighbors can see into the dining room. I love that definition of "naughty." I'd like to meet her someday.

When I call this weekend, have some advice for me. Life is more complicated but a lot more fun with four older sisters instead of one. I feel very lucky.

Love you always, Chap

Chapter 19

By the middle of July, there were no more phone calls coming from California. Instead, there were calls, texts, and pictures flowing into Virginia from Illinois and Missouri. Catherine and Peggy were all settled in the studio apartment in the country. The visit in June had been a total success. They'd loved the apartment, and their landlords, Elaine and Ed, had fallen in love with Peggy, after at first expressing doubts about having a child there.

Elaine said, "It's not a very big apartment."

But then Catherine explained that they were living basically in one room in California.

"She'll have to be supervised when she's in the yard since the cars go by so fast on the road," Ed said.

Catherine answered, "I'll certainly do that, gratefully, since she hasn't been outside much in San Diego, except at the beach."

By the time the agreement was reached with a handshake, Catherine and Peggy had seen their lovely farm pond with a sandy beach and a dock for kids to jump off of and met Elaine and Ed's youngest granddaughter, eight-year-old Katie, who lived just a few miles away. She and Peggy would ride the same bus to school in the fall.

Catherine said to Chap one evening on the phone, "I think I've made the right move for the first time in my life."

They'd arrived in their car, stuffed with only their clothes, bedding, bath linens, and books. Part of Catherine's planning had included weighing the cost of a rental van with simply replacing the few items of furniture she had in their California room. They unpacked the car and made a quick trip to the closest grocery store to buy food for a couple of days. That night, they spread their blankets on the floor and slept in their new apartment for the first time.

Catherine's first purchase was a new bright-blue pull-out couch— "So you can come visit," she said to Chap. Then at two different used-furniture stores, she found a cherry wood desk and chair, a small table and a chair for Peggy, matching dressers and twin beds, a round oak dining table with four chairs, and a bright red area rug. Her only other big purchase was a television set.

"I adored my roommates, but it'll be nice to choose what I want to watch on television some of the time—at least not unless *Sponge Bob Square Pants* is on," she said with a laugh.

Catherine was already signed up to do substitute teaching in the county when school started in the fall. "Two or three calls a week will be enough to get us by until I can land a full-time job somewhere in the area," she said. "If I'm a good sub, I'll have a foot in the door when someone resigns or retires."

Meanwhile, Marilee's reports were glowing. She adored her landlady, whom she called Aunt Liz since that was what everyone else in the area called her. She enjoyed the outdoor work at the farm. She liked her job in the family-owned restaurant. And she loved having Catherine and Peggy just ten minutes away, especially with a pond where they could swim and picnic when the Illinois weather became oppressively hot and humid. She was looking forward to her classes in the fall. And on top of everything else, she'd managed to pet Mozart three times without him hissing at her.

* * *

By the end of July, everyone had motel reservations in Missouri for the wedding—three coming from Virginia by car and three from Illinois. The five Smith siblings would all be in the same place for the first time since Chap was five years old.

Greg was an only child, raised by his mother. His father had rarely made an appearance in his life. He hadn't been asked to the wedding because, as Greg said on the phone one night, "We don't even know where he is."

That night Chap thought about what Greg had said about having an absentee father. Chap's father had become absent in a way, but he'd always tried to be there. It was getting easier for Chap to remember his father without the painful lump in his throat. He liked getting to know his father and mother better through his sisters' stories. His father had triumphed in so many ways. He hadn't followed his own father into alcoholism and despair which had ended in suicide. He hadn't followed his mother into a listless, depressing life style. Instead, he'd created the foundation for all five of his kids to want to be good, successful adults— with some bumps along the way for Marilee and Catherine—and he'd left money to help them all pursue their dreams. Chap thought his father would be very happy to know that soon all of them would live close enough to each other to become a real family again—in no small way, thanks to him.

* * *

They drove across Maryland on I-68, following the same route Lori and Chap had used when they'd gone to Illinois almost exactly a year earlier. Then at Morgantown, they headed southwest on I-79, which took them to the capital city of Charleston where three interstates intersected and numerous bridges crossed the Kanawha River. On I-64 west, they left the city behind. Winding their way through hills—tall ones yet but definitely not mountains—they crossed the rest of West Virginia. The hills in Kentucky gradually got shorter with more grass and fewer trees as they proceeded west toward Lexington. They stopped there for the night with about two-thirds of the trip behind them.

The next morning, after a big breakfast of pancakes, sausage, and eggs, they headed for Louisville where they crossed the Ohio River on the Sherman Minton Bridge into southern Indiana. The highway wound its way west, passing through the Hoosier National Forest, which made Chap ache for the woods he'd known so well near Riverwoods.

The landscape became flatter as they drove into Illinois where corn and soybeans grew in great abundance and the occasional pasture was dotted with livestock. There were no large cities beyond Louisville, just green exit signs for towns with unfamiliar names every ten miles or so.

Doug and Lori took turns driving while Chap dozed or gazed out the window in the back seat. As the miles slid by the car window, Chap thought about his future. He was still feeling torn about moving before he graduated from the Academy or being separated from Lori and Doug until he did. Doug's parents had offered to let him live with them while he finished school. The question was whether or not he could manage another upheaval in his life. It'd been two years since his world had first been turned upside down. He remembered the day Lori had come home early from work and fixed a special dinner for him and their father. He was fifteen and a half then. While they ate, using the good china and silverware, she'd announced that she was being transferred to

Virginia for a few months. Then when he was sixteen and a half, they'd left Indiana for good. The house had been sold, and their father was in the VA hospital in Illinois. Now at seventeen and a half, he was facing another big change, but what would it be? The pieces of his life were very jumbled.

"How about a rest stop, guys?" Lori said. "There's one in two miles."

Chap was always ready for a rest area, especially one with vending machines full of a variety of snacks not good for him.

A few minutes later, Chap sat on top of a picnic table in the shade of a maple tree, eating a Kit Kat and wondering if soon he'd actually be living in this state, not just crossing. After the wedding, they planned to caravan with Marilee, Catherine, and Peggy to Central Illinois to "scout out" the area, as Lori said.

As Chap walked back to the car, he decided to relax because whatever would happen would happen. Until then, he'd just try to enjoy every day, and this particular one in Illinois was easy to enjoy since it was sunny and breezy and beautifully green.

* * *

The motel room was packed. Chap and Peggy were sprawled across the foot of one of the king-sized beds with Catherine and Marilee at the head, their backs resting on pillows. Lori sat with Doug's arm around her at the head of the other bed with Julianna sitting yoga-style at the foot. Greg sat in the only chair in the room, facing them all as if trying to fathom this family he'd be joining in less than twenty-four hours.

Everyone was full of pizza, salad, and bread sticks and pleasantly tired. It'd been a busy day. Chap, Greg, and Greg's Uncle Cliff had shopped for matching tan slacks and summer shoes. Greg had already purchased short-sleeved white shirts with fancy white embroidery down the front. Catherine, who would be the maid of honor, had gone with Julianna to find an appropriate summer dress that would complement her wedding dress, which no one was allowed to see. Everyone else had spent the day exploring the small state park near the town south of St. Louis where Greg's grandparents lived.

Now the four sisters were laughing themselves silly with do-you-remember-when stories while Chap, Peggy, Doug, and Greg mostly listened.

"Remember when you climbed the tree," Julianna said to Catherine, "and then apparently forgot where you were and stepped off the branch to watch an airplane."

"Yeah, that cost me a broken arm in an itchy cast and no swimming for the rest of the summer." She shook her head. "You've got to be pretty awkward to break both arms in one lifetime."

"Wasn't that the day that Mom and Dad made two trips to the emergency room," Julianna said to Lori, "because you slid down the bannister and split your head open when you flew off the end?"

Lori said nothing, just pushed up her bangs to reveal the fine white scar on her forehead.

"And what about the time in first grade when you added a leg to your F in reading to make it an A, using a blue pen instead of a black one like the teacher used," Julianna said to Marilee.

"I could read. I was simply tired of those silly little workbooks we had to fill out."

"Well," Julianna said, "if I remember right, you ended up filling out 'those silly little workbooks' every evening for several weeks."

Marilee wrinkled up her nose at her.

"Hey," Catherine said suddenly, looking first at Marilee and then at Lori, "how come these stories are just about us? Was sister number two such an angel as to have no stories we need to tell about her?"

Lori and Marilee said, "Noooo," in long, drawn-out, dramatic fashion.

"Let's see," Lori said. "There was the time Julianna drew a whole barnyard scene with a black marker on the wall behind the couch and signed it 'Chap.'"

"Ooooh," said her sisters.

"I'm not done," Lori said. "When she got caught, she insisted that Chap had done it—Chap who wasn't even walking yet!"

Chap grinned. He'd never heard that story before.

"Then there was the time Julianna picked all the strawberry blossoms in Mom's carefully tended patch," said Catherine.

"Ooooh," her sisters said again.

In mock horror, Greg threw up his hands. "What kind of person am I marrying?"

Julianna hopped off the bed and plopped onto his lap.

"A lovely, artistic woman who appreciates the beauty of white flowers," she said, giving him a big kiss.

"Cool it, you two. There are children present," said Catherine.

Chap jumped up from the bed and strode to the side where Catherine was sitting. Hands on his hips, he glared down at her—all six feet of him.

"Children? Did you say children, as plural of child?"

Catherine slid off the bed and knelt at his feet. "Forgive me, Great Tall Brother."

Everyone broke into laughter.

"Good heavens," said Greg. "You're all nuts!"

The laughter ceased abruptly as all of them stared at him, stony-faced. Greg's normally tan complexion seems to pale right before their eyes, making his dark-rimmed glasses seem even darker in comparison. The grin on his face froze and then faded.

"But nuts is good," he added feebly.

All five Smiths burst into laughter.

"Gotcha!" said Julianna giving him another big kiss.

"How often are we going to have to see all these people?" Greg asked Julianna.

Before she could answer, Lori said, "Really often because Doug and I plan to find a big house in Illinois where we can have Sunday dinners together."

"We are?" Doug said with a deep frown. "*Every* Sunday?"

Lori poked him in the ribs and said, "Another comedian!"

Greg rose suddenly, dumping Julianna onto the floor. "I just remembered," he said, again in mock horror. "Isn't it bad luck for the groom to see the bride the night before the wedding? I think I'd best leave before my possible bad luck becomes awful luck. See you all tomorrow."

Soon after Greg left and the laughter died down, everyone retired to their own rooms. The day before the wedding ended.

* * *

The first of August was a rare lovely breezy summer day without excessive heat or humidity. The wedding was held in a little log chapel near the entrance to the state park. A winding path edged with deep pink rose bushes led to the double doors.

On cue from the organist, everyone inside the chapel rose and turned to watch first Catherine in a pale-rose summer dress and then Chap and Julianna walk down the path and into the chapel.

Julianna was stunningly beautiful in a lightweight white summer dress with a scoop neckline, cap sleeves, and a flared skirt. Her dark curly hair, which was most often pulled back into a bun or pony tail, was hanging loose to her shoulders. Streamers of white flowers hung down her back from a wide comb in her hair. Greg, who was just a bit taller than Julianna, looked into the eyes of his bride with unconcealed adoration. The three o'clock service was lovely with vows written by Julianna and Greg, a short message from the minister, and solos sung by Julianna's best friend.

Afterwards, everyone walked a short distance to the pavilion in the park. Mr. and Mrs. Greg McMunn led the way, arm in arm, with seven more McMunns following—Greg's mother, his paternal grandparents, his Uncle Cliff and Aunt Sarah, and their two sons, who were just a bit older than Peggy. The Smith guests numbered six and the close friends a dozen or so. On a table covered with a pink cloth, the caterer had spread out a picnic supper of ham sandwiches, slaw, potato salad, and a variety of homemade pies. As everyone ate and visited, one of Greg's friends took many photos of the group.

When the sun dropped behind the trees, the newlyweds gave hugs to everyone. Then they got into Greg's old Toyota and left for their honeymoon—destination undisclosed.

* * *

The next morning, the remaining Smith group met in the motel for a continental breakfast of cinnamon-raisin bagels, all kinds of cereals, donuts, fresh fruit, yogurt, coffee, and juices. Then they piled their luggage into two cars and headed northeast. After driving through the city of St. Louis, they crossed the wide, muddy Mississippi on I-70 east. Again Chap watched the fields of corn and soybeans slide by the window, wondering if this flat, often treeless landscape would ever feel like home.

Chapter 20

Journal Entry #12 - August 13

What a summer! We just got back from a trip to Missouri and Illinois. On Saturday, Julianna and Greg got married in a little chapel near a state park south of St. Louis. The weather was beautiful for August. The ceremony was beautiful. Julianna was beautiful. (Guess I'm not in the mood to think of synonyms for beautiful*).*

Sunday we followed Marilee, Catherine, and Peggy back to East Central Illinois. We three got a motel room while they continued on to their homes. We spent one day touring the University of Illinois campus. Then, the next day, we drove to the farm and met Aunt Liz and Mozart, who is a gorgeous orange and white long-haired cat with an evil personality. I couldn't get close to him. Aunt Liz took us on a tour of her garden, which was currently full of tomatoes and all kinds of squash. She proudly showed off her little flock of chickens and her raspberry and blackberry bushes.

Marilee looks so relaxed. She'll be starting GED classes next week in Springside. She played a couple of piano pieces for us, using both hands already—an accomplishment for which she demanded praise. (I had to work to get that sentence not to end with a preposition.)

Catherine's upstairs apartment is great. It has sloping ceilings, windows on both sides, and an outside deck. The sleeping area on the north side is separated from the rest of the apartment with a half wall. There's room for twin beds and two dressers. The bathroom is on one end of that space and a large closet is on the other. Then the living-dining-kitchen area is all open. It feels very spacious, partly because Catherine doesn't own much. A table and four chairs, a desk for her and a table for Peggy, a bright red rug, and a new pull-out couch plus an old rocking chair and a TV stand the landlords loaned her. She's done some decorating with items from yard sales and Goodwill, which has always been Peggy's favorite store, mainly because, as Catherine says, "It's about the only place where I can afford to buy anything."

The landlords are Ed and Elaine. They had a pond party while we were there with their local family, including granddaughter Katie, who is a little older than Peggy, and some neighbors. We ate and swam all afternoon. There was a constant parade of kids jumping off a dock. You know me, usually not very talkative around most people, but I was very relaxed and comfortable all day. Both Marilee and Catherine are in very good places now.

The next day, Lori, Doug, and I headed for Chicago. We met Erica and her parents for lunch somewhere downtown—I have no idea exactly where I was in that huge, beautiful city—and then we walked around for a while before we all piled into their big SUV for a tour of some sights. I'm no fan of cities after living in one for a year, but being close enough to visit Chicago would be great.

Erica said to tell you hi. She is walking with almost no limp now, and she is pain free. After a summer of working at her high school, she says she feels the strongest she has since the accident. Neither of us knows where we'll go to college, but both of us have applied to universities and colleges in Illinois. It was good to see Erica again.

The Academy opens again tomorrow after the two-week summer break. I'm ready to head back. Are you ready for school to start? I know lots of kids don't want summer to end, but I never thought much about how teachers feel.

* * *

Chap didn't elaborate in his journal entry to Mrs. Hunt about how good it'd been to see Erica. His heart had pounded all day as they walked hand-in-hand. Late that afternoon, it was very hard to tell her good-bye, and with four adults on the scene, a kiss was out of the question.

Later, as the changing landscape slid by the car windows, Chap had thought about Erica all the way back to Virginia.

* * *

De was on his knees, his arms folded on the floor, his bony rear end sticking up in the air. Spread out in front of him was a large road map, crisscrossed with blue lines. Owen and Chap were seated at a table nearby.

"We're here," De said, raising himself up on one elbow and pointing to Virginia on the two-page U.S. map, "but you went all the way to here for the wedding."

He moved his finger slowly across Maryland, West Virginia, Kentucky, and Illinois, coming to a stop at St. Louis.

"Then you are going to move up there." He traced the route from St. Louis northeast up to Central Illinois.

"Maybe. Nothing's certain yet," Chap said.

"Then why'd you go there?"

"That's where the University of Illinois is. We spent a whole day walking around the campus. Since summer school had just ended, most of the forty thousand students were gone, so it seemed pretty quiet. We got to see the State Farm Center where basketball games are played and Memorial Stadium just across the street. We also saw the Union Building, which has big white pillars on both the street side and the quad side."

"What a quad?" asked Owen.

"It's a big open grassy area with lots of trees and sidewalks that crisscross it. Great big buildings surround the quad, some really old since the campus was founded in 1867. There are also lots of newer buildings and one of the biggest libraries in the whole country."

"Is that where you'll go to college?"

Chap shrugged. "I've got to finish my high school work here first. Besides, Lori and Doug haven't made any decisions set in stone."

"What's that mean—set in stone?" De asked.

"Well, if you chisel words or numbers into stone, they're going to be there for about forever. Right?"

De and Owen nodded.

"The expression means that when something is set in stone, it's a firm decision."

"So you may not move?" Owen asked, his face brightening.

"No, we're going to move, but exactly where and when haven't been decided. We drove through a lot of towns in the area, some itty-bitty ones with only a few hundred people and some bigger ones of several thousand."

"You're going to be thousands of miles away," De said with a catch in his voice.

"Not thousands," Owen said, hopping off the chair and walking to a pull-down map on the wall of the Social Studies Center. "Look here, De."

Owen was working on a U.S. geography unit about the fifty states.

"See, it's not like he's going to Oregon or Arizona or even Alaska," Owen said, pointing to those states and showing off his newly acquired knowledge. "He's just going from the East Coast to the Midwest."

Apparently somewhat comforted by this display of a distance less than thousands of miles, De picked the map up off the floor. "I need a snack before I get back to work."

"And I need to go see Miss Sydney about graduating," Chap said.

* * *

With Chap's Riverwoods transcript and his Academy records spread out on her desk, Miss Sydney made some notes on a form. Finally, she looked up at Chap.

"On the plus side, your ACT score is very good even though you took it before you were quite finished with geometry, and you're very close to meeting the graduation requirements for English, social studies, history, music, and foreign language. On the other hand—"

When Chap immediately moaned, Miss Sydney laughed.

"It's not as bad as all that!"

"I know. But it's math. More math."

"Right you are. It's more math."

Chap grimaced. She laughed again.

189

"You can likely be done with all your classes except math and science by mid-September. Then you can concentrate on finishing the chemistry course. Math, however, is a bit of a problem since you need to finish the geometry course and then complete the advanced algebra course."

"I could be done by Christmas?"

Miss Sydney frowned. "That's too optimistic. Spring break is more realistic. What I recommend now is that you finish all the course work for the five classes I mentioned and take the final exams. Then you can put more time and effort into science and math. To get more time, you could quit tutoring. We'd allow that since your circumstances are special—needing to move with your family."

"Oh, no. I want to tutor. That's the best part of the day," Chap said.

Miss Sydney smiled. "Why am I not surprised? You're a favorite with the younger kids here. I hope you do decide to go into education. Male role models are needed, especially in elementary schools."

"Thanks," Chap said as he stood up. "I can do this."

* * *

By mid-October, the fall weather in Virginia was perfect. The air was warm in the daytime and crisp at night without the city smells. Trees were blazing in all the colors of autumn, just like the ones so prominent in Chap's memory of the Indiana woods.

As Miss Sydney had predicted, Chap had finished all his course work for English, history, social studies, and music. He'd also managed to finish geometry with an almost perfect final exam. He'd be taking the Spanish final next week. He was about half way through the chemistry course, and he'd started the advanced algebra work the previous week. He'd accomplished all that without giving up tutoring or spending time with the babes and little ones in the nursery a couple of times a week.

Doug had been seriously job hunting. He'd tweaked his resume in August, which was being sent by email and snail mail to lots of places. He'd flown to Illinois twice in September for job interviews.

October 14 had come and gone without anyone mentioning the significance of that date though Chap was sure that Owen was aware that his life had changed very dramatically just one year before. Lou Ella's condition had stabilized. Miss April or Mr. Allan took Owen to see her in the nursing home every few weeks. Chap had gone twice. Even though she couldn't walk or speak, Chap was certain that her eyes brightened whenever she saw Owen, and she raised her hand off the arm of the wheelchair to greet him. Mollie had never come to see either Owen or her mother.

Then on October 30, Lori announced at the supper table that Doug had news—"Good news," she said.

"I've got a job in St. Dennis with a start-up tech company."

"That was fast," Chap said.

"Very fast," Doug replied. "I have to start in less than two weeks."

Chap's eyes widened as he gulped. He started to say "What!" but instead he forced a smile and said, "That's great."

"Thanks for trying to be happy about this," Doug said. "I appreciate that. Lori and I have known about this for a couple of days—long enough for us to figure out what to do. Here's our plan."

At this point, Lori took over the explanation. St. Dennis was about half way between Prairie City on the west and Springside on the east.

"Doug has already found a room to rent in a small town close by. He'll leave next week. You and I'll stay here until you're finished at the Academy."

"You can't do that!" Chap said, staring at both of them.

"Yes, we can," Doug said. "I'll be close enough to Marilee and Catherine to see them once in a while. Besides, we already have tickets for you two to fly to Illinois for both Thanksgiving and Christmas. Lori will come next spring when the weather is better to look for a house for the three of us. We'll all be together after you graduate from the Academy."

"I can't let you do this! You shouldn't be separated because of me."

"Hey, Little Brother, I'm your guardian for three more months—"

"Not *three*," Chap said, interrupting her.

"All right, not *quite* three more months," Lori said, wrinkling up her nose, "but I'm pulling rank anyway. This is what we've decided."

"You'd better mind her," said Doug, leaning over to whisper in Chap's ear. "You know how she is."

Lori swatted him with a folded up newspaper that had been lying on the table.

Chapter 21

It was exactly as Chap had pictured—the whole family, all eight of them, sitting around an old oak table elongated with two leaves, finishing a traditional Thanksgiving dinner. After everyone helped to clear the table, carrying dishes into the large kitchen with the huge butcher block table in the center, his sisters shooed the guys out of the kitchen and into the living room where Peggy was already asleep, curled up in a big easy chair. As his sisters' voices and laughter floated from the kitchen, Chap settled into the other easy chair.

Greg and Julianna's house was a two-story 1950s bungalow located on a tree-lined street in Prairie City. The previous owners had done a complete remodeling about ten years earlier. All the original charming features of the house were still there, just spruced up— the high ceilings, the pocket doors, the wood plank floors, the bay window in the living room, the river stone fireplace. The kitchen and the bathrooms both upstairs and down had been totally redone. A wall separating the living room from a dining room had been removed so that room was now large enough to accommodate Greg's grandparents' baby grand piano at one end and the large oak table at the other. There was a master bedroom downstairs and two spacious ones upstairs, each with a sloping ceiling. The house felt both old and homey but with some features of a new one. Chap hoped Lori could find such a place for them.

That night there was, in Peggy's words, a "slumber party." She and Chap slept on couches in front of the fireplace while everyone else slept in the three bedrooms. The next day was full of card games, Scrabble, Bananagrams, a jigsaw puzzle of hot air balloons, and football on television while everyone talked, still filling in all the missing years.

After a lot of hugs and a few tears, Marilee, Catherine, and Peggy left late Friday afternoon for the trip back home, which was about ninety minutes for Marilee, who lived the farthest away. Lori, Doug, and Chap stayed one more night.

The next morning after breakfast, they left as well. The plan was to spend some time in St. Dennis, driving around different neighborhoods and the downtown area, before Lori and Chap's Saturday evening flight home. They were hoping to avoid the massive crush of air passengers that often flew on the Sunday after Thanksgiving.

Doug decided to zig-zag through the country on a two-lane county highway instead of taking the interstate back to St. Dennis.

"It's more scenic," he said.

A light snow had fallen on Thanksgiving Day, and it had stayed cold enough for the landscape to remain unblemished. The drive was beautiful with snow on the top side of branches and snuggled onto the gray-green evergreens here and there. Corn stubble poked up through the snow, but the bean fields were mostly white.

They rounded a gentle curve and crossed over a small creek on an old bridge with metalwork crisscrossed above it. Just beyond the bridge, they passed a white house situated on a small rise.

"Stop!" Lori yelled.

"Why?" Doug yelled back.

"That's my house!"

Doug slammed on the brakes and pulled onto the shoulder. He stared at his wife as if she'd suddenly lost her mind.

"It's for sale!" she said, her eyes wide.

"What do you mean?"

"There's a for sale sign in the yard. Go back!"

"You're serious?"

"That's my house!"

"I don't get it," Doug said, his forehead creased with deep frown wrinkles.

"When I was little, I used to dream of my own special house. That's my house!"

"Lori, we're not ready to buy a house. Let's be practical here."

"Please, Doug. I've seen my dream house only from the outside. I've never known what it would be like on the inside. It can't hurt to look."

Greg gave his wife another long look, but when she seemed to be totally sane, he pulled into a lane up the road and turned around. Slowly, he drove into the gravel driveway that looped around the house. Lori flung open her door, raced up the side steps, and crossed the porch.

Doug said loudly as he and Chap stepped out of the car, "I sure hope people don't shoot strangers in this part of the country!"

Behind him, a voice said, "No, sir, not in this part, at least."

Chap and Doug whirled around. Lori stopped in front of the door—her fist, which was ready to knock, suspended in air. A short man with a grizzled gray beard and striking blue eyes stepped away from a large spruce tree and walked toward them. He was wearing an old red-and-black plaid coat and a Cardinals baseball cap. A string of Christmas lights was in his left hand.

Smiling, he extended his other hand to Doug. "I'm Clarkston Jones. And who are you?"

* * *

Two hours later, Lori laid down the legal pad she'd borrowed from Anna May Jones, a petite lady with huge glasses and bright red fingernails. Her gray hair was pulled back into a low pony tail and tied with a paisley bow. Anna May poured mint tea into mismatched coffee mugs and placed slices of pumpkin pie on delicate china plates.

They'd toured the whole house and the half acre property. Lori had taken voluminous notes and asked many questions.

Now it was Anna May's turn to quiz them. She wanted to know all kinds of things: Why did they want to live in the country? How was Chap related to Lori and Doug? Did they have jobs? Why were they living in two states? Were they planning to have children? Had they ever owned a house before?

Even though she didn't ask, Chap was sure she wanted to ask if they would love this house as she and Clark had for over forty years.

Lori had all sorts of facts written down. The closest town, Flatland, was big enough to have a post office, two restaurants, one bar, one barber, two hairdressers, a bank branch, a fire station, and a convenience store-gas station where "you can get milk and bread but not hamburger or eggs," Anna May said. "You have to plan when you live out like this."

She nodded with approval when Lori explained where they'd lived on First Woods Road. Lori knew all about weekly trips to town to run errands and grocery shop.

"It's an easy drive to St. Dennis unless the weather's bad," Clark said.

Lori had lots more on her legal pad. The creek had never risen high enough to flood the basement. The well had been redone about twenty years ago along with the septic system. The siding and roof on the house were fifteen years old, the furnace and central air eight. The three-car garage and woodworking shop behind the house had been added when

Clark retired. There was a small garden patch behind that and even a fenced area with a chicken coop though they didn't have any hens at the time.

Chap thought the house seemed old enough to feel settled but new enough to be nice, just like Greg and Julianna's. There were two large downstairs bedrooms, one of which was cluttered with Anna May's craft and sewing projects. The living room-kitchen area was all open with only a bar separating part of it. The kitchen had recessed lighting that shone softly on light oak cabinets. Upstairs were two big bedrooms with sloping ceilings and a dormer window in each. On the back wall were built-in closets and storage space as well as a small bathroom.

It was the special touches that Lori seemed to notice. Louvered doors hiding the washer and dryer in the kitchen. A large walk-in pantry. A brick fireplace with built-in bookshelves on both sides. Four double windows across the front of the house, two on either side of the front door. The spacious porch that went across the entire width of the house. The wrought iron rail. The steps on either end that led down to flagstone paths that curved around to the back of the house. The flower beds and shrubs in front of the porch, along the sides of the house, and around the old iron wheels at the ends of the circular driveway.

As they sipped the tea and ate pie, Doug was almost afraid to say what needed to be said, but finally, he explained that they wouldn't be moving to Illinois until late spring or early summer.

"Perfect!" Clark said.

"Perfect?" Doug responded.

"Yes. Our son is building a cottage for us on his property in Tennessee, and it won't be done until March. We almost didn't list the house now because we were afraid if it sold right away, we might have to move twice."

Lori grinned. "I knew this was supposed to happen. I just knew it."

Suddenly, she looked at her watch and stood up. "Oh, we've got a plane to catch!"

There was a final flurry of questions and answers and the exchange of phone numbers.

"We'll be back at Christmas," Lori said, giving Anna May and Clark hugs.

"I'll have it all decorated by then," Clark said as he picked up the lights he'd laid down on a chair. "We'll see you then."

* * *

Buying a house seemed to be terribly complicated. Chap was glad he didn't have to be involved beyond giving his approval to the plan. He watched from the sidelines. When Doug called, Chap heard references to "realtor, mortgage, and escrow"—whatever that was. On her end, Lori did lots of research about the area, especially about the new consolidated school complex which housed K-12 all on one campus. The answer to Anna May's question about having kids was apparently yes. She looked into nursing schools in the area and part-time jobs. She researched both universities and colleges all over the state for Chap and even a couple of community colleges.

Lori was absolutely certain that they needed to look no further for a house. Doug, on the other hand, was less certain. Several times a week, he sent her pictures and descriptions of houses for sale in the area. Lori managed to find fault with each one—the lot was too small, there weren't trees in the yard, there was no basement, the kitchen was ugly, it was on a busy street, the shutters were the wrong color, the bedroom windows were too small.

In early December, Julianna and Greg drove to the house for "an inspection," as Anna May called it. The house passed with flying colors.

Marilee and Catherine gave it a thumbs-up after seeing the pictures Julianna took.

Lori loved "her" house in the country, and Doug loved her. The preliminary papers were signed on December 27th. They were soon-to-be home owners.

Chap thought it was funny that his address had once been Riverwoods, where he'd lived in the woods with Wandering River close by. Now his address would be Flatland, another accurately descriptive word for the landscape.

Chapter 22

When Chap entered the Academy on Monday after the winter break, he was ready to live and breathe algebra with just a little time out to tutor in the Language Arts Center and to do the laundry.

As Chap sat down to listen to two young boys read, he saw De deliberately trip a five-year-old girl. Chap jumped up to intervene, but since she landed in a beanbag chair, there were no scrapes or tears, just a very angry stare at De's back. Chap sat back down. The next day, Owen didn't come prepared for his math work and refused to make it up when his tutor tried to help him. That afternoon, De smeared peanut butter in a boy's hair in the lunch room, and Owen knocked over his cranberry juice and left the puddle for someone else to clean up. Wednesday morning, De took a seat in a beanbag chair and sat for the entire day, arms folded in defiance, as he'd done when he'd first come to the Academy. Owen did all of his written work incorrectly and then joined De in a beanbag chair that afternoon.

Miss Sydney was watching the boys, but so far she seemed to be following the Academy's practice of trying to let things work themselves out. Then Thursday morning, Miss April waved a white flag of surrender. She asked to meet with Chap and Miss Sydney in the eating area, away from where the boys were still on their sit-down strike in the yellow and purple beanbag chairs.

With frown wrinkles replacing her usual smile, she said, "What on earth is going on with those two? We haven't got a clue, but something is really wrong!"

She proceeded to describe what had been going on at home. Several times they'd hidden Leeza's favorite stuffed cat and made scary faces at Rose until both girls cried. They totally quit saying "Please" and 'Thank you." They shoved their toys and books into a closet rather than picking them up and putting them on the shelves as they'd done before. They left puddles and soppy towels on the bathroom floor after showers and quit taking their dishes to the sink after meals.

"None of their actions are really terrible when considered one at a time, and they've done nothing to physically hurt Rose or Leeza, but this sudden change is very worrisome."

After Miss Sydney and Chap detailed what they'd been observing, Miss Sydney said, "Let's see how tomorrow morning goes. Can Mr. Allan come by before lunch if we need to talk to the boys?"

"He can."

Since the next day was the first Friday of the month, all January birthdays were being celebrated in homeroom, including Owen's and Chap's. As usual, there were oranges and bananas in three baskets and two big plates of peanut butter cookies. Cards for all seven kids with January birthdays lay on the table.

Chap felt like he was on high alert, wondering if anything was going to happen. He didn't have long to wait.

In a split second, De swept the cookies and the baskets of fruit off the table. Chaos ensued as some of the little kids cried and the bigger ones yelled at De, who was standing like a statue, staring at the shattered glass plates, the broken cookies, the baskets, and the fruit all over the floor. Then Owen grabbed the seven birthday cards off the table and ripped each one in half.

Without a word, Miss Sydney grabbed both boys by the arm and hustled them into her office. Once they were seated in chairs on opposite ends of her office, she closed the door. Quietly, she asked Chap to stay in the center for a while to help her keep an eye on them. The older kids were already sweeping up the glass and cookie crumbs, and some of the younger ones were refilling the baskets with fruit. A couple of eight-year-old girls laid out the pieces of the birthday cards and proceeded to tape them back together, even Owen's.

Once everyone was back on task, the morning routines began. Though Miss Sydney appeared to ignore the boys, Chap knew she was sneaking peeks at them through the glass wall of her office.

Two hours later, Miss Sydney, Chap, and the O'Neills sat in a semicircle around the two boys who were now in chairs close together.

"All right, you two, explain," Miss Sydney said.

There was silence.

"We're waiting," she said.

The silence got longer and longer. De began to fidget, and Owen's face was turning red.

Then Chap said quietly to Owen, "Remember what keeping secrets can do?"

That seemed to break down the barrier, and once Owen began to talk, so did De.

"I don't want to be adopted," Owen said, tears welling up in his eyes.

"Me neither."

Eyes wide, Miss April asked, "You want to move to a different foster home?"

"Oh, no, we want to stay with you," De said.

"Yes," Owen added, nodding his head vigorously.

"Okay, guys, you've lost me here," Mr. Allan said. "You don't want to move, but you don't want to be adopted, so that means you must want to stay foster children."

The boys nodded.

"Now I'm lost," said Miss Sydney. "What does all of this have to do with you breaking the rules here?"

De's face lit up as if someone had finally asked the right question. He looked back and forth between Miss April and Mr. Allan. "If we're bad, you won't want to adopt us and make us your *real* kids."

Unable to contain his surprise, Mr. Allan's eyes widened, but Miss April simply tightened her lips to suppress a smile as she said, "That makes sense, but maybe you'd better tell us what's wrong with being adopted."

"I can't lose my name," De said.

"What do you mean, 'lose' it?" said Mr. Allan.

"My grandpa showed me pictures of him when he was a little boy. He was skinny and blonde like me. He told me that I was an Ellison just like him, so I can't be De O'Neill."

"And I'll be the last Barsky when my grandma is gone—at least I think so."

Chap knew what Owen meant. His mother hadn't contracted him, not even on his twelfth birthday.

It was the O'Neills turn to nod their heads. "I see," said Mr. Allan. "The problem is changing your names if you're adopted."

The boys nodded again.

"Well," he continued, "the idea is that if we are all O'Neills, then we'll seem more like a real family—you two, Leeza, and Rose along with our older sons. But maybe there's a way to compromise."

"What's *compromise* mean?" De asked.

"It means to figure out a way to make everyone happy," Owen said.

Both boys looked at the four people sitting in front of them, waiting for a compromise, hoping maybe to be happy.

Chap spoke first. "Owen, I've never asked, but do you have a middle name?"

"No. I'm just Owen Barsky."

"Could you be Owen Barsky O'Neill instead?"

Before Owen could answer, De shouted, "And I could be De Ellison O'Neill!"

Both boys grinned.

Suddenly, De frowned as he said to Miss April and Mr. Allan, "We're happy, but Owen said everyone needs to be happy. Are you happy, too?"

They smiled.

"Guys, I think before we go back to work, we should talk a bit more," said Miss Sydney. "You know that you were unfair to others here and at home just because you were trying to solve a problem. What would've been a better way to solve that problem?"

"Talk to people first?" Owen offered quietly, looking at Chap. "Get the facts."

"Right. Now can you make this up to those you were mean to?" said Miss Sydney.

"You mean 'pologize?" asked De.

"Yes, apologize," said Miss Sydney. "It's simple to say to someone that you're sorry, but you have to mean it."

The boys sat with eyes downcast.

Then De's shoulders began to shake. "It was all my idea," he sobbed. "I had to tell Owen how to be bad 'cause he's never bad by himself."

Mr. Allan reached out to hold his hands. He said, "But Owen went along with you. That makes him also responsible."

It was Owen's turn to cry. Tears leaked out of his closed lids and slid down his cheeks, "I didn't have to do the bad stuff. I'm the older brother. I'm supposed to know better."

Moments later, Miss April said, "You know, this past week hasn't been much fun at our house, but when you love someone like we love you boys, you don't quit loving them—even when they're acting bad. Your actions *were* bad, but you boys are *not* bad."

Then, in a rush of words, both De and Owen made promises about apologizing to their classmates and cleaning up at home and using manners and reading stories to Leeza and Rose and using their allowance to buy new plates and peanut butter cookies for everyone in homeroom and doing all their schoolwork again.

Miss April and Mr. Allan hugged the boys. Miss Sydney and Chap grinned, and the escapade ended.

* * *

January 19

Dear Erica,

I know that I haven't been writing letters since I doubled up on my school work last fall—with your permission, that is. But today feels special, so I want to get some ideas down on paper for a change—though I've loved talking to you more often on the phone.

Eighteen is just a number, but my eighteenth birthday is a big one since Lori is technically no longer my guardian. I can make choices for myself, but the odd thing is that I don't want to. I want to start over again in Illinois. I want to move to that little house in the country. It's funny that it seems like a "little" house since it has four bedrooms, but compared to our house on First Woods Road, it is little. I hope that it'll feel like home soon and not like a place where I have a bedroom.

At Christmas, we spent time there again with Clark and Anna May, who have sort of adopted the lonely Doug. They've been inviting him to supper every once in a while, and then they play a card game called *Golf.* Doug has promised to teach it to Lori and me. Anyway, Lori has now measured every room and every closet and drawn a floor plan to scale. Anna May has even given her pictures of the flower beds in bloom so that Lori will know what perennials to expect next spring—"If they all survive the winter," Anna May said.

As I told you on the phone, Christmas was a lot of fun. I don't think I told you about our gift exchange. Since all of us, except Greg and Julianna, are sort of in transition, we'd decided to go easy on the gift buying. Marilee bought everyone scratch-off lottery tickets, which all bombed except for Peggy's which turned out to be worth 25 dollars! "That's a shopping trip to Goodwill for more winter clothes," Catherine said. Julianna and Greg gave us all tins of homemade cookies. Catherine bought everyone some sort of "smell pretty," as Peggy said—cologne or shower gel or aftershave. I got everyone a paperback book. It was fun to figure out a different one that each might like. Lori and Doug gave everyone two pairs of funny colorful socks.

Maybe the best part of it all was planning our family get-togethers for the rest of the year. We have a written schedule of who, what, and when that includes a party for Marilee and me since she'll get her GED about the same *time as I get my diploma from the Academy, a couple of pond parties, some Sunday dinners, and time together for the holidays, of course. Does it seem possible that just two years ago, I wrote that paper for Mrs. Hunt entitled "Loss"? At that time, I had no sisters at home and no mother. Even the heron I liked to watch had migrated south.*

I told you about all the drama with De and Owen not wanting to be adopted. It's funny how kids can get an idea and then decide on what to do. There was a sort of logic to what they did! I wonder if anyone else noticed something Owen said. He referred to himself as the "older brother." That sounded so good to me. He's going to be part of a family that's not "dysfunctional." Remember him saying that to me when I first met him?

The adoption proceedings have begun. Miss April hopes they'll be faster than last time since they've already been through the system with Leeza. It's not like the boys have anyone else to take them in. De with no living grandparents, a mother who died when he was four, and a father sentenced to life in prison. Owen with no known father, a missing mother, and a totally disabled grandmother. And no one has ever come forward to claim Baby Rose, who was abandoned at a fire station.

Owen one time told me that the O'Neills were the first real family he'd ever met, even if they looked "funny." When I asked him to explain, he said that Miss April is" kinda black," meaning she's light-skinned, and Mr. Allan is Irish with red hair. One of their sons has his mother's coloring and the other has his father's. Then there's five-year-old dark-skinned Leeza and Baby Rose, who is pale with rosy cheeks and reddish-brown curly hair. We all need to quit calling her Baby Rose since she's been walking since Christmas! Anyway, they'll be adding a tall skinny eight-year old with whitish blonde hair and a short dark-haired twelve-year-old with a curved spine. Owen does have a point!

At home, I'm just plugging away. Lori spends a lot of her free time "arranging" our furniture with her pencil and eraser on the scale drawing of the new house. I know she misses Doug terribly, but she is putting no pressure on me.

Chemistry will be done by the end of the month, and then I will only eat and sleep and do algebra for who knows how long. I feel torn. I really love the Academy and a lot of the kids there, especially De and Owen, but I'm ready to leave, ready for the adventure of college, and, most important, ready to be closer to you.

With all my love, Chap

* * *

The first hints of spring began to arrive—three robins in the yard one morning, several crocuses up in the flowerbed, rain showers instead of snow flurries, and people walking their dogs in the neighborhood in light-weight jackets.

Erica had been accepted at four universities in Illinois, but she hadn't yet made up her mind where to go. Out-of-state tuition for Chap was going to be a major cost, so he wasn't sure what he intended to do either.

Lori was still planning the move so that she'd know where every single item they owned would go. She flew to Illinois in mid-February to sign more papers.

Then things sort of fell apart again.

* * *

I can see the end. The end of algebra, that is! I should've earned all my credits for a high school diploma by spring break. Two of my classmate will, too, so we'll be a graduating class of three. Actually, every few months, a group graduates. Since kids don't all start at the same time or go the same number of days each year or work at the same speed, they're leaving the Academy all during the year. The same is true with kids coming in. There's no beginning date for a bunch of five or six-year-olds to enter kindergarten. Instead, every month or so, one or two or three new kids are introduced to our homeroom—like when De and I arrived on the same day. Some are just starting school, some are moving up from being little ones, and some are older kids like me. They just get absorbed into the routine that basically runs itself. Anyway, this isn't what I wanted to tell you about. It's Owen.

About a week ago, he seemed suddenly to be very quiet. He was unenthusiastic about his class work, even lethargic. Miss April and Mr. Allan were quite worried, but he wouldn't talk to them. Anyway, Miss April asked me to take a shot at getting him to open up since we've always been close.

After homeroom the next day, Owen and I borrowed Miss Sydney's office. I told Owen that when people change suddenly, it usually means that something is wrong. I reminded him of how simple it had been to solve the name problem just two months before, once the O'Neills knew what was wrong. I said that he could trust me to try to do whatever was best for him no matter what the problem was now. As I talked to him, he looked like he had when he'd first told me about Nelson Nelson—all shrunk up and withdrawn with dark circles under his eyes. Finally, he let it all out with lots of tears.

It's quite a story. Apparently, a week or so ago, Owen saw a front-page feature story about some badly decomposed remains which some workmen had found under an overpass. The story's focus was on how difficult it often is to identify such bodies. In this case, just bones, hair, and teeth were left. The coroner said the body was that of a female in her late twenties or early thirties. The hair was naturally dark but had been dyed blonde. The only other clue, according to the article, was a necklace—a large silver M—which was shown in a photo.

You've guessed it. Owen recognized his mother's necklace.

Between sobs, he explained why he hadn't told anyone. He was afraid that he'd have to identify the remains at the morgue. I think he used to see a lot of CSI type television with Lou Ella. Apparently, he was having nightmares about seeing her skull with hair attached.

You know, Owen is so smart and serious about learning that I forget how young he is—just twelve. Anyway, Owen had decided to keep the secret, but it was eating away at him.

To make a long story short, I went with the O'Neills and Owen to see Detective Jarvek since we'd worked with him after the attack by Nelson Nelson. DNA from Owen was used to verify that the body was Mollie. Since the coroner found no evidence of trauma, the cause of death was listed as undetermined which will likely be changed to accidental overdose once toxicology reports are in. Did you know that hair can indicate recent drug use?

Then I went with Owen and the O'Neills to tell Lou Ella, but we aren't sure she understands that her daughter is dead. I'm sure that Owen is mourning in his own way, but Mollie had had almost no influence in his life since he was born. He'd always lived with Lou Ella, who was a somewhat indifferent caretaker.

Now, once again, there is peace at the Academy! The idea that I have been there to help Owen and De—neither one was dealt a decent hand for years—makes me even more convinced that I want to do something with kids. Since I will be leaving soon, it makes me feel good to know that they are now in the best of hands with Miss April and Mr. Allan.

* * *

Then it was graduation day at the Academy. There was no "Pomp and Circumstance" played by a school band. No group of nervous graduates. Instead, the day before the two-week spring break was called the Chap, Chuck, and Shannon Day. During homeroom, the three graduates donned bright blue mortarboards and gowns, which they would wear all day. At noon, there was a special lunch table for the three of them and iced cookies for the entire school population. All day,

Chap smiled and shook hands with all the big kids and little kids who congratulated him as he made his last rounds of the centers. At two o'clock, he posed for his senior graduation picture which would be added to the book of graduates at the Academy along with an autobiographical sketch that he'd written himself.

At three o'clock, the hard part came. He sat down the Owen and De, who'd shadowed him all day. Miss Sydney took pictures. They exchanged email addresses. The boys promised to study hard so that they could wear a cap and gown at the Academy someday. Then there were hugs and tears that didn't quite overflow. Chap was now an Academy for Mutual Instruction graduate.

* * *

This time there was no big yellow rental van. Instead, the professional movers arrived at eight o'clock with all kinds of packing materials and proceeded efficiently and swiftly to empty the rental house, room by room. Lori and Chap had packed just one suitcase each for the car trip. Aside from that, they would have just the vacuum cleaner and some cleaning supplies in the car. Three hours later, the van pulled away from the house, taking most of their worldly possessions with it.

Chap and Lori stood in the middle of the bare living room, surveying the emptiness.

"All right, Little Brother, let's man the mops!"

"I'll start in the bedrooms," Chap said.

"Don't forget to wipe down the ceiling fans and the tops of the door frames. I expect this landlord to give us the white glove treatment, and I really want our security deposit back."

"Yes, Sergeant, Ma'am, Sergeant."

Lori wrinkled up her nose and pointed at the vacuum cleaner.

Two hours later, the landlord knocked at the door and inspected the spotless rooms. Smiling, as she pocketed the check for the refunded deposit, Lori handed him the keys to the house.

After taking a quick shower, Chap loaded the two suitcases along with the cleaning supplies. Then they were off.

One more chapter of his life had ended.

Chapter 23

May 3

Hi, guys, how are things at the Academy?

I'm attaching some pictures of the new house in Illinois. Ask Miss Sydney to show you how to look at them. It's really pretty here now that the trees, the grass, and the fields are turning green. We've been very busy getting settled in. At the last minute, Lori decided to repaint almost every room in the house since she's not a big fan of yellow. The upstairs bedrooms and bathroom are now a light green. Their bedroom and bath downstairs are two shades of tan. The kitchen is a very pale robin egg blue, and the living room is ivory. Then Lori decided to replace all the drapes that were left here with window blinds, so now all the natural woodwork around the windows shows. But I guess you guys aren't much interested in house decorating.

I'm practicing driving with Doug. Living way out in the country is really different from where you are. If you don't have a car or a truck, you stay home. No buses. No taxis. I had a license for a short time in Indiana, but I'm really out of practice after two years of being a city kid like you. I'm going to look for a part-time job once I get my license and a car, which I'll need to get to school.

I've decided to start at a community college. If I go there two years, my credits will transfer to a university in Illinois. My sister Marilee is going to a different community college about two hours away from mine. I hear that the men's basketball team is better at my school than hers.

Lori and Doug say hi. I really miss you guys. Write me back when you have time.

* * *

"I've got news!" Lori said as they sat down to eat supper.

"You always make me nervous when you have big news," Chap said.

"Why is that?" said Doug.

"Well, the first time, it caused her to desert me for months and months, and the second time she dragged you to Indiana."

Chap grinned and ducked as Doug swung at him.

"No, really, I have some good news. I got a job today, part-time. The pay isn't much, but the hours are flexible enough for me to continue working when I start school in the fall."

"Where?" Doug asked.

"At the library in St. Dennis."

"Have you ever worked in a library?"

"Does being a library volunteer in high school count?"

"Nope, since I'm guessing you did it to get out of study hall."

Lori grinned. "So what did you do to get out of study hall, Mr. Perfect."

"Lifted weights."

"Hey, that's what I did, too," Chap said, giving Doug a fist bump.

"Anyway, I start Monday, which means we need another vehicle unless Chap intends to stay home alone."

"Not a chance. Like, duh, how do you think I'm going to get to summer school?"

"I still can't believe you miss the Academy so much that you want to go to summer school here, too," Doug said.

"I got used to going all the time, I guess."

"Hey, guys, back on topic—we need another car," Lori said, eyebrows raised. "I have an idea."

"Beware of ladies with ideas. We guys generally come out on the short end of things," said Doug.

Ignoring Doug, Lori said, "Chap gets my *old* Honda, and I get a *new* one."

"I get Old Gray with 165,000 miles on her?"

"Right, and she'll be cheap—cheap enough for someone without a job," Lori said with lots of emphasis on *without a job*.

"Like I said, we guys get the short end of things, but Old Gray is better than nothing, right?" Doug said to Chap.

"I guess so. At least I know that she runs."

* * *

June 6

Dear Erica,

Another anniversary of sorts. Two years ago today Lori and I moved into the apartment in Alexandria. If it weren't for the Academy, I think that time would've been really awful. This country boy didn't like city life, but inside the Academy, it didn't feel like a city at all—just a community of kids.

Summer school is good, so far. I have three classes that are required for an associate's degree. The college is accepting my music classes for college credit, and I tested into the third level of Spanish. I'm thinking about minoring in Spanish since knowing that language is likely to be beneficial for many kinds of jobs.

Now I'm taking rhetoric, American history to 1865, and psychology. Classes are long since the summer session lasts only six weeks. We meet Monday through Thursday, so it's go to class almost all day and then study all night.

It does seem odd to be back in a traditional school with big classes of twenty to twenty-five, specific daily reading assignments, due dates for papers, and announced quizzes and exams. And grades. Most of mine are good so far, but I totally missed the point of an opinion piece we had to read for rhetoric and got a D on the paragraph response. The instructor wrote on the paper what I'd done wrong, but I didn't rewrite it to show that I now get the point. Instead, there's a D in her green grade book that will be figured into my average. It seems so strange to just go on without correcting an error like that.

I think I've really lucked out with the three instructors since you hear about professors who simply appear in class and lecture for the duration, droning on and on. The rhetoric instructor mostly illustrates how to handle various writing assignments and there's a lot of discussion about the controversial articles we read. She's already praised my "near-perfect use of grammar and mechanics." Thank you, Mrs. Hunt! The history class is covering a lot of what I learned at the Academy, just more in depth since the literature part is missing. Thanks Academy! Psychology is new, and I really like it. We write a lot of short responses to various readings. It's a lot of work, but I like to write. Enough about school!

I'm so excited that you've decided to go to the University of Illinois. Yes, I admit that it's because you'll be closer, but I really like that huge beautiful campus. I hope to join you there some day.

I've landed a weekend job which I should be able to keep next fall. Really exciting—stocking shelves in a grocery store in St. Dennis. Just me and the boxes. I was trained in about half an hour. "Don't block the aisles. Don't slice yourself up with the box cutter. Learn where everything is so you can help customers"—no one has even asked me a question yet—and "put the new stuff behind the old stuff."

I'm paying Lori monthly for Old Gray—reminds me of your dad's truck you called Ole Blue—and I need money for gas and insurance. By going to the community college first and then transferring, I should be able to get my bachelor's degree without any debt, thanks to my share of the inheritance. Glad to hear that you have two scholarships. I always knew you were smart like me. (Did you just stick out your tongue at a letter?)

Even though I called the apartment and the house in Virginia home because Lori and Doug were there, I knew that both places were temporary ones, not like what home was in Indiana. Now I have a great upstairs room with all my old stuff. It's at least twice the size of my room in Indiana—with a dormer and a view across the front yard which is now green. I've counted seven deciduous trees and five large evergreens on the half acre. It's really very pretty with lots of flowers. Even so, it doesn't feel like home yet, and I don't know why?

When can you come down for a visit? I want to tell you all about the guys in Riverwoods. Going there with Lori for graduation weekend in May was great fun. I always thought of the guys I hung out with as sort of lackadaisical, but they all have great plans for their futures. Tom has joined the Navy. If you're wondering where a kid from Indiana got the idea to go to sea, his explanation makes sense. When his dad lost his job last year, his parents had to use most of their savings to keep their house. Anyway, Tom wants to see the world and then use the military benefits to pay for college later. Troy is going to Purdue to become a pharmacist, Jason is going to join his father in farming, Deon is attending Ivy Tech in criminal justice, and Jack is taking training to build and repair wind turbines—says he'll be a master mechanic, just one who works two hundred feet in the air!

I'm driving now, but Lori says I'm not ready to tackle Chicago highways and traffic, so please come see me! I miss you.

Love you forever, Chap

* * *

It was close to midnight on July 3rd. Chap was staring at the sloping ceiling of his room, remembering some of the nights during his last year in Indiana when insomnia had ruled and his stomach hurt. Now his stomach didn't hurt, but his heart was pounding despite the fact that he was lying motionless. Even though he'd become more verbal during the past couple of years, Chap still often planned his words carefully before he spoke. At that moment, his mind was a jumble of words he needed to form into some sort of coherent message. It was time for them to talk.

He pictured the bedroom next door—the pale green walls, the blinds that were most often raised half way up, the moonlight that was throwing white light on the bed, the dresser, the old rocking chair rescued from the attic in Indiana, the small sofa, and the corner table decorated with Lori's Uruguayan collection of whimsical cats and dogs. All of that Chap could see in his mind's eye.

What he couldn't picture was Erica. Was she asleep? Or was she also awake, thinking about him as he was thinking about her, wishing that there was no wall between them?

Chap remembered when he'd first seen Erica—only her back when she criticized his autobiographical paper one morning in English class at Riverwoods High School and then her scarred face when he rejected her friendliness on First Woods Road the next afternoon. Then there were all the days for the next two months when he ignored her until the afternoon when she held him close after his father had hit him in the face for the first time ever. What followed were six wonderful weeks when they saw each other every day—until he crossed the line and touched her in a way she didn't want to be touched. Then she was gone, back to Chicago for more surgery on her leg.

There had been letters and more letters and many phone calls, but they'd seen each other only three times in the past two years—at the house on First Woods Road right before Chap and Lori moved to Virginia, at the VA hospital in Illinois when his father was dying, and in Chicago for an all-too-short afternoon.

Chap had been in love with Erica for almost three years. What he desperately wanted to know was did she love him, too? She had often reminded him that they were too young to think about a future together. That might've been true when he was not quite sixteen, but he was older now, and he ached for her. But how would he tell her that?

* * *

Chap awoke suddenly when the sun shone in the east-facing dormer. He tried to grasp the dreams of Erica, but they slipped away as dreams so often do. He lay still, watching the pale shadows of the trees dance on the ceiling. She was really asleep nearby. That he knew was not a dream.

Erica had driven down from Chicago in time for dinner the night before—a dinner of grilled T-bones, baked potatoes, and salad made of fresh-picked spinach from Lori's little garden. The four of them had played Bananagrams for a couple of hours before Lori and Doug called it a night. When Chap kissed Erica good night outside the guest room door, she hadn't said, "Don't be lonely," as she'd said in the past because this time she wasn't leaving. She would be there in the morning.

With that thought, Chap bound out of bed, grabbed clean clothes, and tiptoed past the closed guest bedroom door to the bathroom. Ten minutes later, as he was tiptoeing past the door again, Erica poked her head out and said, "My turn?"

Chap's heart thudded. Even with tousled, uncombed hair and sleepy eyes, she was beautiful. Any words he'd planned to say to her evaporated, and he mumbled, pointing to a cupboard door, "Clean towels in there."

After a breakfast of bacon and Lori's famous scrambled eggs, Chap asked Erica if she felt like taking a walk. When she said yes, he grabbed a small backpack which he filled with four water bottles, some granola bars, and two oranges.

The day was warm and breezy without the humidity so often prevalent in mid-summer in Illinois. They walked down the road a short ways to the bridge that crossed the creek. Chap was quiet as they leaned on the metal railing which was covered with rust spots and peeling dark green paint.

This little creek had no name, and it didn't gurgle over rocks since it was only inches deep in early July. Compared to Wandering River, it came up quite short. Chap was still having trouble feeling at home. It seemed that he kept comparing this place with his home of sixteen and a half years in Indiana. His big room lacked coziness. The view across the front yard seemed to be more human-created rather than nature-made like the Indiana woods.

"Not like Wandering River, is it?" Chap said, breaking the silence.

"Not really," Erica said, "but I do see a little school of minnows."

"Where?" Chap asked.

Erica pointed to a shaded place directly beneath them. Then, looking up, she said, "Have you explored the creek yet?"

"What's to explore?"

"Well, it looks like it goes into that patch of trees in the distance. Maybe there's something back there."

"We'll be trespassing once we go beyond the back side of our property."

"Chicken," she said, wrinkling up her nose at him as Lori so often did.

"I'm not going to pay your bail when we get arrested."

Grinning, Erica grabbed his hand and pulled him away from the bridge.

The going was fairly slow since the mid-summer grass along the creek bank was knee high, and in places willows grew in thickets which had to be skirted. The occasional raspberry cane snagged on their shirts. Within ten minutes, sweat was rolling down their cheeks.

The first birds Chap spotted were red-winged blackbirds—the males with the bright red bars on their wings and the females with the buff-colored ones. Chap continued to identify the birds he saw. A female cardinal, a meadowlark perched on an old hedge fence post, a pair of brown thrashers scratching along the edge of a field, a kingfisher with its oversized head and little body, and several gold finches. Erica was impressed.

"I can't identify much beyond a robin or a cardinal or a sparrow," she said, pointing at a little brown bird.

"That LBJ isn't a sparrow," Chap said.

Erica raised an eyebrow. "LBJ?"

"Little Brown Job. You aren't a real birder unless you can identify all the various little brown birds, too. The one you pointed to is a female gold finch."

Erica laughed. "How come you know all about birds?"

"I completed several ornithology units at the Academy."

"Why did you choose to study that?"

"Because some smart aleck girl in Mrs. Hunt's English class once humiliated me by pointing out that I didn't know the difference between a crane and a heron!"

Erica scoffed. "Hardly humiliated since no one knew you wrote that paper except Mrs. Hunt and you. I only guessed."

"But I was deeply wounded," Chap said, clutching at his heart.

"Pathetic," she said, grinning and shaking her head.

Then she took the lead and proceeded on toward the trees in the distance.

Erica was right. There was something in the little grove of trees. They didn't need any archaeological training to recognize evidence of human habitation. Old bricks outlined the shape of a house, and a pile of rotting lumber included two old doors, weathered to a soft gray with their glass knobs still in place. Chap found a pile of broken bottles and dishes and a few totally rusted tin cans that crumbled at his touch.

"I wonder who lived here, and why did they leave?" Chap said.

"This was home to someone for a long time," Erica added.

After walking around the property, they sat down on the slightly sloping top concrete step of three which had once probably led to a front porch shaded by towering maples but which now led up to nowhere. Chap opened the back pack to get out two water bottles and the granola bars. Neither spoke for a while.

Finally, Chap said, "We need to talk, or I guess I should say that I need to talk."

"All right. About what?"

Chap took a very deep breath, but he didn't know where to start. All his planning during the night was for naught.

As the silence got long, Erica said, "May I guess?"

Chap nodded.

"You want to know if I'm in love with you."

Chap stared at her. It would've taken him paragraphs to get to the heart of the matter.

"How did you know?" he stammered.

"Chap, you've hardly been subtle. Think of how you sign your letters," she said with a smile. "You wrote about your sisters' weddings in detail, even said you pictured me coming down the aisle at Lori's wedding. You told me about working with the babes and little ones at the Academy. That hardly sounds like a guy not interested in love and marriage."

"Transparent, huh?"

"Definitely."

Chap waited for her answer to the question, but an answer didn't come. Instead, she said, "I've dated a couple of guys in Chicago—you know that. None of them are anything like you, and they come up short in comparison. Maybe it's because of how you grew up without the usual set of parents, I don't know, but you seem so much older than eighteen. You have an idea of what you want to do. You care about so much more than just yourself. You don't have a rocky relationship with your family. You aren't rebellious—you know, smoking or drinking or notching your belt with—well, with you know what. You're just different."

Chap's heart was pounding in his ears. "Is different good or bad?" he finally said.

"Different is good, definitely good."

Chap continued to wait for the answer to the question, which hung in the air like a motionless balloon.

Finally, Erica spoke again. "Everything I know about you I like, but we've actually spent very little time together during the almost three years since we first met. I wonder if you *really* know me—with all my quirks and sometime bad moods and scars both inside and out. And do I *really* know you?"

Chap's heart thudded louder, but now it was from fear. Was he losing Erica?

"We've kept a long-distance friendship going for over two years. That's pretty remarkable in my book," Chap said. "It's true that I don't know everything about you or you about me, but I worked closely every day with girls at the Academy. We laughed and talked as we worked, but I never had any feelings for them like I have for you. I'm very sure that I love you and that I'll always love you. Whatever differences that come up we'll solve—if you love me."

"And if I do love you, what will happen next?" asked Erica.

"What do you mean—'what will happen next'?"

"I guess I'd better just say it—sex. Do you want to have sex?"

Chap's eyes widened. Any words he might've said flew right out of his mind. Did Erica know what he'd been thinking about last night? Did she know that he'd pictured her lying beneath the sheet—remembering the one time he'd touched her breast, remembering her anger, remembering her accusation that he was being nice to her only to get sex because how could anyone really love her with a scarred face and a crippled leg?

Erica was staring at him with her beautiful deep-sea-blue-green eyes.

Finally, Chap spoke. "The truth. Yes, I've dreamed of having sex with you almost since that day when you held me as we stood along First Woods Road. For God's sake, Erica, I'm a normal guy!"

Erica smiled.

"But if you're asking me if I expect to have sex right away, the answer is that we'll decide together when the time is right. Do I hope it's before I'm thirty? Yes! But I'm willing to wait."

Erica stared at him, as if having to process that idea. Then, looking very serious, she said, "Do you sleep naked?"

Chaps eyes got very wide again, and his face burned.

Erica grinned. "Sorry, but you seem to be so very proper sometimes, and I was trying to imagine how you looked in your room so close to mine last night."

"Well," Chap shot back, "you'll just have to wait to see how I sleep! And maybe you will be thirty!"

Erica laughed. Standing up, she pulled on Chap's hand. Then, facing him, she put her arms around him. "I think I love you, but I want to get to know you better. I want to be sure about us. I want sex to be an extension of real, long-lasting love. But, in truth, I doubt if we'll be anywhere close to thirty—"

Chap stopped her with a kiss.

Then, hand-in-hand, they continued to walk along the creek, but when they found nothing unusual beyond the old home place, they turned around and headed back toward the house. It was getting hotter, and there was a lot planned for the July 4ᵗʰ holiday. All the Smiths were coming for an afternoon parade in St. Dennis, an evening cookout back at the house, and fireworks in Prairie City. As they made their way through the thick grass, Erica admitted that she was nervous about meeting three more Smith sisters, Peggy and Greg, too.

"What if they don't like me?"

"Well, if I tell them you picture me naked, they'll be shocked!"

Erica punched him in the arm.

Rubbing his arm, as if in great pain, he said, "But if I tell them only about your kind and gentle nature, they'll love you."

"You are no help!"

He grinned at her.

About half way back to the house, they spotted an old wooden plank bridge, probably once used to cross from one field to another. There were big holes in the wood. Stepping gingerly to test each board before putting their full weight on it, they moved onto the bridge and sat down on the side. Away from the willows, they could feel the breeze. Sitting quietly, they drank the last of the water and ate the oranges. It was very peaceful. Beyond the occasional tree along the creek were cultivated fields. The corn was over two feet tall, but the soybeans, which had been planted later, were just starting to turn the fields solid green.

Suddenly, a movement in the sky caught their eyes. A heron was approaching, its wide wings flapping lazily up and down, its neck pulled back in an S-shape. It dropped lower and lower until it was flying just above the water. Then it landed gracefully on a low willow branch that stretched over the creek.

Chap and Erica hardly breathed.

It's all here, Chap thought. All the pieces of what had made up home were actually here, too. As the breeze cooled his face, he drew the contrasts. The old house in the woods which changed with the seasons, the new house surrounded by fields that would also change as seeds sprouted and plants matured and then dried before harvest. A wooden bridge over a river, a metal bridge over a creek. Living with his father and Lori, a quiet family of three; living with Lori and Doug, two very special parts of a lively family of eight. Erica, who was his friend then; Erica, who said she loved him now. And finally, a heron—there was even a heron here.

Moving in slow motion, Erica reached over to take Chap's hand. "Now are you home?" she whispered.

Chap could only smile at her.

Author's Note

Generally, a work of fiction does not need an end note since the story simply ends as this one does. In *All the Right Pieces*, the characters, the plot, and most of the settings are fiction.

However, there are a few real parts that need mentioning. One of those is the YAK Phonics program, which was created in the late 1960s by my father as part of his UCLA doctoral thesis. While I was working on the final draft of this novel, my sister and I sold the copyright for YAK to a man who is going to upgrade the material. At this time, I do not know about the availability of the program.

Another real part is the Twin Rivers series that Catherine mentions to Chap while they are at the zoo. Those three books were written by my son, Todd E. Creason: *One Last Shot, A Shot after Midnight,* and *Shot to Hell.* I know those books well since I was the editor for those entertaining mysteries as well as two delightful collections of short biographies of famous Masons.

What is really important in *All the Right Pieces* is the Academy for Mutual Instruction. Such a school does not exist, but my teenaged granddaughter said, when she read part of the unfinished manuscript, "I want to go to Grandpa Mac's school!"

Grandpa Mac was Dr. Edwin M. Swengel, her great-grandfather and my father (1917-2010). He was a man of many talents. He was an accomplished musician who created a community orchestra, the Fithian Farmhouse Filharmonic, which became well-known enough to play some USO shows at Chanute Air Force Base in Illinois and to be featured in a farm magazine in the 1950s. He farmed the acreage that my mother had inherited. He turned an old one-room school house surrounded by ten maple trees into a large sprawling home in which my husband and I still live. When my family moved into Little Giant School after World War II, the blackboard was still on the back wall and the only bathroom facilities were the boys' and girls' outhouses.

But most of all, my dad was an educator. He spent years searching for ways to make our schools better. While working on his master's degree at the University of Illinois, he became interested in Maria Montessori's methods—he earned his master's the same year I earned my bachelor's there. That summer he went to California to take Montessori training and then, after returning, co-founded a Montessori school in Champaign. Shortly after that, he, my mother, and youngest sister moved to the Los Angeles area where he became a Montessori principal and later entered UCLA.

Dad's real passion was his ideas for restructuring schools totally to allow for individual differences in a way that the current system of one teacher for a group of same-aged kids can never do. He believed that the answer was Mutual Instruction where kids learn how to tutor each other.

He chose in his later years to present his ideas about restructuring schools in novels. His first venture was *Plainston Chronicles, 1919-1951,* published in two volumes. He was working to complete *Conspiracy,* which is set in the city of Plainston in later years, when he died at age ninety-three. With my sister Marcia's blessing, I finished that manuscript as its co-author.

On one of my many trips to visit him and Mom in California, I read to him an early draft of *All the Right Pieces*—the part when Chap first goes to the Academy. He said, "That sounds like my school," and I replied, "I hope so because that is what I intend."

At the beginning of *Plainston Chronicles,* Dad wrote, "The author regrets that all characters, events and places in this book are fictional. This story *could* and *should* have happened—but did not." I repeated that in the introduction to *Conspiracy* because he is right.

I have created the Academy for Mutual Instruction based on his and my ideas about how such a school might be structured. The school would be based on a number of general concepts that most of us educators as well as parents accept.

1. Age is often not a good indicator of when a child is ready to start school.
2. Kids are social beings.
3. Younger kids often look up to older kids.
4. What we teach we learn even better.
5. Kids in a same-age class can have a wide range of abilities. I know! I remember a 7th grade reading group I once had in which the reading scores on an achievement test from the previous year ranged from 2nd-11th grade.
6. In a traditional classroom, some kids are so far ahead that they are bored. Some are so far behind that they are discouraged or frustrated or even angry. Kids from both groups may become discipline problems.
7. In a group setting, a lot of student time is wasted since some kids could move more quickly and some aren't mastering skills because the pace is too fast.
8. Failing grades most often do not motivate kids to do better. Most often those low grades act to discourage them.

In case you've decided that I am a Pollyanna, I will tell you that I have spent forty years teaching in traditional classrooms, including this current semester at a community college where I am teaching developmental reading in a classroom with desks in rows, a set curriculum based on a textbook, and a department final exam all must pass after thirty-two days of class—and that some will not, despite my best efforts and theirs. I have never taught in a school even remotely like the Academy.

However, I've come to believe that if children were in multi-aged groups beginning when they were *first* in school—expecting to be tutored by older kids and then learning to tutor younger ones later themselves— that such a school could work. I also believe that many teachers would relish an environment such as the one at the Academy, that a year-round school is a good idea, that parents would support such a school where students could truly work at their own paces and where progress reports would replace grades.

Dad died before finding a combination of parents, teachers, and supporters who would create a real Academy. I'm convinced that someday there will be such a school because the concepts he espoused in his novels and on which I based the Academy for Mutual Instruction in *All the Right Pieces* deserve to be tried.

About the Author

Jane S. Creason lives with her husband, Don, in a remodeled one-room schoolhouse in Illinois, where she has lived since she was four years old. There they raised their two children, both married. Six generations of her family have lived in that schoolhouse or visited there regularly, including now their four grandchildren and one great-grandson. Jane earned her bachelor's and master's degrees in secondary English education from the University of Illinois. She has been a life-long teacher in East Central Illinois. Her career has been unusual since she taught at the grade school, middle school, and high school levels before retiring. Since then, she has been a part-time English instructor at a community college. Jane's hobbies include reading and writing, gardening and mowing, working crossword puzzles, helping her husband sell his antique collection, walking in the country, and spending lots of time with family and friends. Though she enjoyed the many trips to Southern California to visit her family over the course of forty-six years, she loves the Midwest with the changing seasons and the small farm where she has spent most of her life.